Treason in Eswy

BOOK TWO

Treason in Eswy
THE WARLOCKS OF TALVERDIN

K.V. Johansen

Library and Archives Canada Cataloguing in Publication
Johansen, K. V. (Krista V.), 1968-
Treason in Eswy / K.V. Johansen.

(The warlocks of Talverdin; bk. 2)
ISBN 978-1-55143-888-7

I. Title. II. Series: Johansen, K. V. (Krista V.), 1968-
Warlocks of Talverdin; bk. 2
PS8569.O2676T74 2008   jC813'.54   C2007-906660-7

Summary: In this second volume of the Warlocks of Talverdin series, Maurey, the Nightwalker
prince, helps young Princess Eleanor combat a plot by her enemies to take over the kingdom.

First published in the United States 2008
Library of Congress Control Number: 2007940127

Orca Book Publishers gratefully acknowledges the support for its publishing programs pro-
vided by the following agencies: the Government of Canada through the Book Publishing
Industry Development Program and the Canada Council for the Arts, and the Province of
British Columbia through the BC Arts Council and the Book Publishing Tax Credit.

Cover artwork by Cathy Maclean
Typesetting by Christine Toller

ORCA BOOK PUBLISHERS   ORCA BOOK PUBLISHERS
PO Box 5626, STN. B   PO Box 468
VICTORIA, BC CANADA   CUSTER, WA USA
V8R 6S4   98240-0468

www.orcabook.com
Printed and bound in Canada.
11 10 09 08 • 4 3 2 1

*For Marina and Susanna, who remind me why I write,
and for my sister April.
She knows why.*

The author gratefully acknowledges the New Brunswick Arts
Board, for a Creation Grant which assisted
in the writing of this book.

CONTENTS

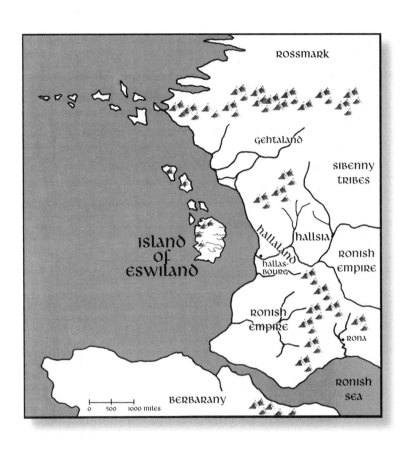

Prologue

This is our history, written not for the historians, but told for our descendants. Read it, so that the story of those days is not forgotten. Remember it, so that what we built will endure, protected and honored by those who come after us.

Maurey, Prince of Talverdin

PART ONE

✣ CHAPTER ONE ✣

KORBY: AMBUSH

The following account of the treason in Eswy was given by the Moss'avver, Korby, sworn man of Prince Maurey of Talverdin. It was set down in his own words by Mathilda Clerk, Scholar of Asta College at the University of Cragroyal, at the request of Maurey of Talverdin, who says that, as a spy, the Moss'avver never had to encode his reports, since special training is needed to read even his signature. The Moss'avver has many skills. Fine penmanship is not one of them.

Whoever they were, they were good. We never heard them coming. I never even *felt* them coming, not till it was too late.

That night my lord and I had broken into the library at Hallasbourg University, scaling the high walls and getting in through a window to the gallery—not for the first time. The library was a long chamber divided into dozens of alcoves by ranks of shelves, which thrust out like ribs from the walls. There must have been at least several thousand books, plus all the pigeonholes holding ancient scrolls and unbound manuscripts. The numbers still astonished me.

Soft footfalls went on ahead, while I paused, listening. The prince's steps and my own breath—nothing else.

The shuttered lantern I carried cast a dim golden light ahead of me as I held it high. Pillars supported the vaulted roof, and a gallery ran around three walls. In some of the alcoves were carrels, high-sided writing desks. A few of these had their own shelf or two, closed with a locked grille; masters and librarians of the university were allowed to keep books important to their studies shut away for their own private use. Taking them out of the library was forbidden.

Master Arvol had been taking them, although stealing books wasn't why we were spying on him. We'd been sent to find out what he was researching. Alchemy, philosopher's secret arts, secret weapons—we didn't know. We made lists of the books he had locked in his carrel, but so far, we hadn't found a pattern.

The prince was ahead of me, at the other end of the long chamber. White light, cold as moonlight but far brighter, sparked to life and rolled into a knot by his head. I could see him pulling books from shelves, opening them to read a page or two.

I turned into the alcove where Master Arvol had his carrel. There were only a few volumes behind Arvol's locked grille now, half as many as there had been last time we were here. I didn't see what we really wanted, a little bundle of unbound pages. The ambassador's agent had reported that Arvol seemed to be writing a summary of his research, and that report had made the king send Maurey and me to Hallasbourg to find it. I set the lantern on the desk and slid its door open a little farther to shed more light. With my hand on the lock of the grille, I tried to empty my mind of other thoughts, pushing the nervous edge that comes with such sneaking work aside, pushing all the questions out of my head. Pushing…

The lock turned with a click, loud in the silence. It was enough to make Maurey start back towards me. I could feel him: the quiet tension that goes with such work as ours, the patience and the calm that made him the man he was.

All of a sudden I felt sharp fear and anger slamming into me, the emotions of a crowd of men, afraid and nerved up for battle. They hadn't been there a moment before; they had been hidden, and that wasn't possible. Unless they'd been in the halfworld—not possible, not for humans on their own.

It hurt, like getting kicked in the stomach, but I'd have been dead long before if I let the pain of the mind slow me down.

"M'lord!" I shouted a warning as I flicked the shutter of the lantern closed. The light made me a target. In the space of a breath, I had my back to the shelves on the other side of the bay, sword and long dagger drawn.

Then they were on me, and I barely had time to notice the strangeness of their weapons. I slashed almost blind at the nearest moving shape, and my blade rang skittering on steel beneath a master's black gown. I caught and swept aside a downward blow with my dagger as yellow light bloomed—one of them had opened the shutter on a lantern like my own, raising it aloft on a pole. Useful. I kicked a man in the chest. He reeled backwards, caught himself on a shelf. Three of them, and they were all human. I couldn't say if they were really masters of the university or not. They wore black gowns, but so did we. The wide-sleeved gown was a useful disguise at night, turning you into a formless shadow, and loose enough to hide armor and weapons beneath.

They were all armed with narrow-bladed swords, but none carried daggers or bucklers. The edges of their weapons were globby, smeared with some thick resin, and it glowed with a greasy white light. The same paste was now scraped over my dagger's blade.

They hesitated. Maybe a six-foot Fenlander armed with a heavy greatsword wasn't what they expected to find in a university library in the small hours of the morning, though they'd come expecting something, that was clear. I grinned, casually swinging the long dagger in my right hand, sword raised in my left. I don't have a pretty face. Scare them enough and maybe they'd back off. There wasn't a lot of room here between the shelves.

A sudden clash and shout told me that there were more, and they had met Maurey. His first impulse would have been to get into the halfworld, but if he thought I was in trouble, he wouldn't stay there.

"Idiot!" I shouted. "Keep out of it! This is my job!"

He wouldn't, of course. He's only passable with a sword, by my standards anyway, but he has other skills. I caught the mutter of hasty words in Talverdine, a spell to put the force of a horse's kick into an open-palmed blow. I'd seen that one before. The red light wrapping around his arm was spooky enough, even before he hit you with it.

A grunt, a thud and a patter of falling books, probably from a body flying into a shelf. That decided the ones facing me that maybe I wasn't the worst thing in the library after all. They were quite right too. I felt Maurey building up walls within himself, shutting off all his emotion—walls of ice, they always seemed to me, deathly cold, adamant hard. You can't let your animal rage at being threatened take over in a fight; you need that cold, thinking watchfulness to stand hand in hand with the long training that has become instinct. But for Maurey, it was a lot more important than just not letting anger give his enemy an opening. Maurey losing control of himself was bloody dangerous to everyone around, friend and foe alike. Maybe the strong old warlocks in the past had known how to control and direct power like what Maurey's had become as he grew to manhood, but nobody did these days, and there was a fire-scorched training hall and a burn-scarred swordmaster in Sennamor Castle because of it. I'd only seen that rage break free once, and it had saved my life then, but it was like one of those eastern alchemical weapons going off, the ones that can bring down a city wall. I never wanted to see it again. Neither did Maurey. Probably these fools were finding facing a calm cold warlock armed with sword and magic quite scary enough.

Two of my three charged again, while the one with the lantern, a plump, dark-eyed blond man—a boy really, only a few years younger than me—stood nervously off, trying to watch for Maurey over his shoulder without turning his back on me.

I feinted at the one on my left, ducked, thrusting up at the one on my right, whose gown I'd already torn. He wore a breastplate beneath his gown, but not full armor—little room for a stroke with full strength behind it, so I went lower. My sword blade struck his hip bone with a sickening grate, and I rolled away to come up with a return stroke that snapped the other man's dainty blade, meant for gentlemen's duels. He ran. I whipped the dagger after him, and he sprawled, twitching. No backplate. Bloody mess. Now we had a corpse to get out of the library.

The boy dropped sword and lantern, shouting in Hallian, "Truce, truce, I'm unarmed!" as he grabbed the wounded man under the armpits and began dragging him.

I don't play polite games with people trying to kill me. I grabbed my own lantern, flicked it open just a crack with my thumb and struck the boy on the head with the hilt of my sword as I went by. He'd live. The one he fell on might too, since the wound wasn't spurting with much pressure. No saving the third one, though.

Maurey seemed to be all right for a moment, back to a pillar, two men lying senseless, one circling nervously at a safe distance. I set the lantern on the floor, retrieved my dagger and turned the dead man's head for a better look. Blond, brown-eyed—definitely human, and so were Maurey's three. So where had they come from and why hadn't I felt them coming?

I'm a Fenlander witch. Humans don't sneak up on me.

The man wore something on a chain around his neck. I pulled it out. An amulet of some sort, a golden disc with a pattern of concentric circles linked by random lines, all in gold and filled in with blue enamel. Pretty, but not the emblem of any Great or Lesser Power or any noble house of Hallaland that

I knew. I jerked it over his head. It might help us figure out who they were.

"Want a hand?" I asked.

The look Maurey gave me was a bit wide-eyed and desperate. His attacker chose that moment to lunge at him. Maurey dodged, almost too slow, and that was when I realized he was wounded. Not all the sickening waves of pain I was shutting out came from our enemies. Some of it was his, leaking through his cracking wall of icy control.

"Yerku, save us," I muttered, and flung myself at Maurey's opponent. He saw me coming from the corner of his eye and chose to run. I didn't bother to chase him, because the prince slid down on one knee then, the fiery exultation of battle and the wall of ice evaporating together. The air cracked and sizzled around him a moment; he had been that close to losing control.

Under his master's gown, Maurey was wearing a leather jerkin over a quilted doublet. No armor of any sort. Who would bother, for climbing over roofs and crawling in windows to creep around an empty building? But he's used to fighting with sword of war and shield. Maybe that instinct had betrayed him and he'd flung an arm up to protect his head, with nothing but a few hasty folds of wool gown wrapped around it. There was no clean cut, though. It looked to me like it had been a glancing blow from what was only a light, thrusting sword—but whatever that glowing white paste was, it had burned through the gown and the sleeve of his doublet beneath.

And what it was doing to flesh—he slumped against me, teeth clenched. I ripped away the layers of sleeve with my dagger, after hastily cleaning it on leaves torn from a book. Maurey didn't notice the destruction, which shows how bad the pain was. In a long line, the skin was blistered through, black and oozing, and the white poison bubbled and writhed over his forearm like it was some living thing.

"Don't scream," I warned, but he was whispering some spell, nothing I recognized. Words against poison, maybe, or against the pain. I wiped the stuff away with the clean side of the torn sleeve. Blackened skin came with it.

"Arvol's notes?" Maurey asked through clenched teeth.

"Not here—again. He must keep them on him. But we've done enough for one night. No way we can clean up all this."

There was blood on Maurey's sword, so the man who got away was wounded. Would he be coming back with others to collect his comrades dead and injured? Would he rouse the university proctors or the city watch? We couldn't afford to find out.

"Leave that," the prince ordered as I reached for the poison-stained rag of a sleeve, thinking some of the alchemists or philosophers back in Cragroyal might be able to figure out what it was. Maurey broke out in a sweat even as my hand held it near. "It's got something in it, something akin to philosopher's fire."

"Great Powers." I hurled it away instead and gave him a hand up. He leaned on me. "Can you make it out of here?"

"Have to, don't I? They knew they were hunting a Nightwalker, whoever they were. But I can't climb over the roofs, Korby. Can you unlock the doors?"

"Always," I said. One of my useful little skills.

"Then let's go home."

He pulled us into the halfworld, and everything went foggy and colorless around me. There in the halfworld the paste on the edges of those swords glowed with a hungry light. Faint tendrils seemed to crawl off it, reaching for us, half-seen, like trails of fire in the corner of the eye.

Sound was distant, as if muffled with water in the ears, but still I heard a door opening, and felt fear and grief and anger enter the library from the gallery up above. Someone who knew what had happened was coming back, with others. Like with sound and sight, the halfworld lets the whispers of the mind pass in only one direction.

"More of them are coming," I said. "And Maurey, they were in the halfworld, or something like it, before they attacked us. I'd have warned you otherwise. I'm sorry, I didn't feel them."

He nodded. They were in the real world now, whoever they were, but they might not stay there. We headed for the heavy main doors, where we had to slide back to the night so I could bewitch the lock open and let us through. I didn't bother to close the door as the prince drew us into the halfworld again. The mess inside would make it perfectly clear someone had broken in.

But the next day, while Maurey, safe in the Dunmorran embassy, lay in a fever despite his spells and what skill I had in healing, I went out about the city and the university campus to see what I could learn. I would have stayed by him, but I'd done all the good I could. It was the ambassador's lady wife who ordered me away.

"To stop his highness fretting and making himself worse," she said. "Set his mind at ease, my lord, and make sure Arvol doesn't disappear on you now."

Master Arvol didn't seem worried. He left his lodgings late in the morning and went to the university as usual. As usual, when I broke in to search his squalid little room, I couldn't find the sheaf of notes that the ambassador's agent had reported seeing. There were the expected heaps of stolen books, though. On a wax tablet, I scratched down a list of the ones we hadn't seen before. The prince had told me not to rob Arvol, not yet. If he didn't know he was being watched, we didn't want to let him know.

There was no talk of intruders or murder in the library, no whisper of fear or mystery. Whoever our attackers had been, they had cleaned up after themselves. They wanted attention no more than we did.

✣ CHAPTER TWO ✣
ELEANOR: DEATH IN RENSEY

Here begins the account of Eleanor of Eswy, written in her Own Hand, of the late treason in the kingdom of Eswy.

I remember the exact moment my tutor came to tell me my brother was dead. I was perched in the opening of an unglazed window in the half-ruined tower of the Old Keep, one knee drawn up, one leg dangling, as I played what sounded like a wild skittering peasant jig on a wooden cross-flute. The piece was actually a popular tune by the mysterious Rose Maiden. Most of her pieces were much more solemn and reflective, even mournful, like "The Caged Starling" (which Lovell had told me all the young ladies of my father's court were singing these days), but this was a tune one could dance to. My skirts and petticoats were hitched up, showing far too much calf, though it was decently covered in thick brown stocking. I beat time against the stone wall with my heel.

And in a shaft of sunset light from the western doorway, Katerina was dancing, barefoot, with her hands on her hips. Lady Katerina was blond, brown-eyed, and even the high-necked, dark brown gown, plain as a peasant's—plainer, because peasants dyed their cloth yellow and russet, and red and green, and wove plaids and stripes—could not hide her ample curves. I had dull, light brown hair, faded blue eyes and no curves that anyone could notice, unless I took all my clothes off—and what a wicked girl I must be to have such a thought. On top of that I had a face like an ax, some dear lady of my mother's had once told me, when she caught me studying it in a mirror.

"Vanity," she said, "is a sin, child, and the Powers know *you* have nothing to be vain about."

I knew my face was narrow, my bones showing sharply, my nose thin and straight. I knew my eyes were too large and staring, not always modestly half-lidded and downcast. But an ax? An ax could cut. People gave way before an ax. I could wish I had a face like an ax, since I could not be beautiful.

"*What* do you think you are doing?"

Katerina whirled around so quickly she slipped and fell with a smack on her behind. I lost my breath in a feeble false note.

We both stared, horror-stricken. The Old Keep had always been safe, haunted by owls and, so rumor had it, the shades of the restless dead, including a tragic piper who had flung himself from the battlements.

Actually my brother Lovell had made up that particular ghost, to explain the music which sometimes drifted from the ruin. I had to play *somewhere*.

"Such heathen behaviour and at a time like this! I could not believe my ears when a groom said you had been seen on the path to the Old Keep, and to find you here in such a pagan display! I am shocked. Shocked!"

I was shocked that one of the outside servants would have betrayed me. I thought they liked me, unlike the indoor servants, who were all my mother's creatures, or knew whom they had to please.

Katerina picked herself up and curtseyed soberly to Master Sneyth. I slid down from the window ledge, trying to hide the flute behind my back. I hoped he would forget to demand it from me. It was a gift from my brother, as were all my flutes and recorders and all my books on music—*The New Book of the*

Pleasing Art, The Eight Sisters, The Harmony—and in fact every other book I owned, whether history, poetry or mathematics.

Master Sneyth drew a deep breath.

"Princess," Sneyth said, "Your Highness. Your brother…"

"It isn't his fault!" I cried. "He had nothing to do with it!"

Sneyth began again, and I realized the sickly color of his face was not anger after all.

"The prince has…there has been an accident, a terrible accident. Crown Prince Lovell is dead, Princess."

I found myself sitting on the floor with my skirts in a heap around me while Katerina gripped my hands, her Hallalandish accent, hardly noticeable most of the time, grown thick with panic.

"Eleanor! Keep your head down, breathe slowly. Oh, Huvehla, be with me, help me, Lady Weaver!" I could hardly hear her pleas to the implacable Power of Fate because of the heavy roaring in my ears.

The sea, I thought. I hear the sea. Lovell had promised me that before I went up to Dunmorra to be married in the autumn, he would steal me away for a day of freedom. We would take a boat down to the sea and fish for sole over the sandbars.

That was when I started to scream.

I do not remember Master Sneyth scooping me up in his arms as though I were a mere slip of a child. I do not remember him carrying me, howling, out of the Old Keep and down the rough path under the curtain wall. I do not remember his climb back up across the inner bailey and into the Queen's Tower.

I do not remember any of this. I drifted in and out of nightmares. Katerina told me later that Master Findley, my mother's physician, forced me to swallow syrupy poppy wine as soon as Master Sneyth handed me over to the women. I do remember a glimpse of my mother, her face pale and expressionless, watching me. She was not weeping. She would not. Not for Lovell. Not for me. She belonged to the Penitent sect. It was a sin to love and cling to frail human life and so oppose the will of Huvehla the Weaver, the Great Power who held the threads of our lives.

I woke, muzzily, some time later. Candles burned about the room. In Eswy we fear the dark, but Katerina, who had only been in Eswy since the previous summer, seemed to fear it more. She sat in a chair by the bed, a book of meditations on her lap, but she was not reading. Her face was stained with tears. She looked up when she heard me stir.

"They say he fell down the stairs," she whispered, before I could speak, "a judgement of Huvehla for his wicked heathenish ways."

I said nothing.

"They say your father has summoned the barons to meet in council, to confirm you his heir." She frowned. "If he would end your betrothal to the heretic in the north, there would be no doubt."

I shook my head weakly. Lovell had met the Dunmorran king, when he was permitted a term at Cragroyal University in Dunmorra. For a prince to become a student in a foreign land, however briefly, was an unheard-of thing, and Cragroyal University allowed many radical ideas to be debated; there was even a college for women, founded by the scandalous Baroness Oakhold, who frequently dressed like a Nightwalker and was whispered to be the mistress of the Nightwalker prince. Lovell, however, did what he willed. Lovell had urged the match on my father and on King Dugald. And on me.

He had been very persuasive. I hoped my father would not give in. He wanted the Dunmorran alliance as a counterweight to my mother's Hallaland faction and his own barons. I wanted… to be anywhere but here.

My head was still full of poppy-dreams. I remembered flying, music pouring from my throat with no need of my flutes.

Katerina sighed and took up an earthenware cup from the nearby table. "The physician said you should drink this, if you woke."

I wanted to push it away, but my hands seemed almost to belong to someone else, fumbling over the blankets as I tried to raise them.

The poppy wine was sweet and bitter, cloying on the tongue. I scowled and puckered my mouth like a baby refusing its mush, and much of the dose ran onto the blankets and the loose bedgown they had dressed me in. Enough found my mouth that I had to swallow.

"I'll read to you," Katerina said.

I lay docile, her words flowing past me.

"Thus it is not fitting to mourn overmuch for the dead…" The words had been written by Holy Elinda, the founder of the Penitent sect and a great-aunt of my mother, whose namesake she was. "…For, if found worthy, they are freed from the sufferings and cares of this miserable world of the flesh, and if unworthy, they are outcast beyond reach of any prayers. Why should we grieve for loss of the base flesh that clothes us? Should we not strive, all our lives, to loose our ties to the heavy clay of the world which binds us in greed and desire, in fear and weariness and pain?"

I drifted into more nightmares, of Lovell falling down a flight of stairs that never ended, of myself trying to catch him but his body passing through my hands as though I were a shade, of my mother with a skull for a face.

I could not have swallowed too much of the dose, because I woke again. The candles still burned, shorter now, and Katerina was in her usual place in the bed beside me, her breath soft and deep. The black ribbon on which she wore a tarnished silver medallion, an heirloom of her mother's house, lay across her throat, and for a moment I stared, fascinated. I had never had a good look at the medallion, because she kept it hidden under her high-necked gowns and only took it off to bathe. Good Penitents like us did not wear jewellery. An incised line made a pattern a little like a labyrinth. It looked very old. But it was the dark band of the ribbon that fascinated my muddled imagination just then. It separated her head from her body. Suddenly I felt horribly ill, seeing her lying there beheaded. I couldn't bear to stay near her. What if I pushed her, and she moved, but her head did not?

Without any conscious plan or desire I rose and slipped out from beneath the covers. Katerina did not stir. There was no water in the jug, and the nightmare faded. Katerina was merely sleeping, hidden in shadows. My mouth felt coated with tar, my throat burned, and the room swayed gently around me. I could not remember for a moment why it should. My feet seemed never to have felt a floor before. How strange. I should send Katerina to find a page to bring water. But I did not want to disturb her: That much lingered from my waking nightmare. I took the jug myself and wandered from the room. The corridor beyond stretched for half a mile and rose slowly up and down in waves. It seemed perfectly natural that it should. A stairway. My heart lurched in fear. Why...oh. I sat down at the top of the stairs. They went down forever, into darkness.

Someone was humming a tune, a lament. It was me. I must be quiet. Music was a vanity; it glorified the human who produced it, not the seven Great Powers. It was gilding on the rot of the world, silk wrapping the corrupting corpse. I wanted a flute, the low, velvet sound of the largest of my cross-flutes, which Lovell said was made of some wood from distant Berbarany, almost at the bottom of the world. Lovell had given me that one only two weeks ago, a spring-welcoming gift on Fuallin-day, the first day of the month, when the peasants (and everybody but Penitents) celebrated that the land was green and growing again. It was bound with bands of silver that he had ordered inscribed with the roses of our family badge. I could hear it blending with the high keening note of the descant recorder. Something to ease heartbreak. My hands twitched to the fingering, but the small locked chest that held my pipes and books was hidden in a dark corner under a different flight of stairs, balanced on the bracing of a beam. Someone was still humming. Still me. I put a hand over my mouth. Was I dreaming? Yes, perhaps. I would not act so strangely, if I was not dreaming.

Poppy wine, I thought. Poppy wine gives you dreams.

I wanted to find my mother and have her put her arms around me as she had when I was small. No, that was Nurse, and she had gone away long ago.

Water. I was looking for water. I remembered.

I found myself climbing down the stairs, one hand against the wall, the jug forgotten.

The stairs turned a corner. At the bottom, faint light gleamed from my mother's private parlor. I sat down again three steps from the bottom, defeated in my quest for water and too weary to climb the mile of stairs back. My head throbbed and whirled, and I wondered if I would be sick.

Perhaps my mother was grieving, and I could comfort her, and we would hold one another and weep like family.

"Sawfield has sent three times in the past month, bargaining for Eleanor," my mother said, speaking Hallian, as she usually did, "and again this very afternoon, with my son's body not yet cold."

"It *would* save the child from her father and from Dunmorra." The voice was that of Dame Hestor, my mother's Mistress of the Wardrobe and close friend.

"Sawfield is luxurious and self-indulgent. He desires the hollow power of the world, but he does not have true humility before the Powers."

"He will stand against the evils unloosed in Dunmorra. He has said so."

"He will say whatever gives him the crown. No, Hestor, we have little time. My husband arranged the Dunmorran marriage to spite Sawfield's ambition, at my—at my heretic son's urging. I know nothing happens except by Huvehla's will; I do not question that, but at the same time, I am weak enough to ask, how could I have borne such a child of evil? But Hiram is too weak to withstand the barons, who will have Eleanor married to Sawfield before the summer is out now that she is heir. But I will let neither my husband nor Sawfield have her. It is not only the crown, but her immortal soul they would seize."

"Can we reach a ship?"

"I have already sent men out. They report that Sawfield's liveried men are all through the port. We would be stopped. Have you begun the arrangements for moving the household, as I requested?"

"I have, Your Grace, but if not home to your brother in Hallasbourg, then where?"

"Two letters," my mother said. "I have written two letters. One is to the Baron of Sawfield. I tell him I will give his honorable request for my daughter's hand the attention it deserves, but that she is devastated by her grief and requires a period of mourning."

"That's true enough." Dame Hestor sighed. A tear slid down my face. I felt quite sorry for my mother's poor daughter, snared in such plots. Ah, my drugged mind remembered, that is me. Poor child.

"We are withdrawing to Narmor Castle in the west. There we will offer prayers for my son's soul and pray for Fescor to carry his shade to Geneh—"

"Madam!"

"I know. To pray for the dead is self-deceiving. Huvehla's will is done. But it is the Eswyn way. We will do it. Huvehla will forgive us, understanding our reasons."

"Yes, madam."

"And at the end of Morronas month we will give Sawfield his answer, and all the necessary arrangements will be made for Eleanor's wedding."

"You make no reference to the king, madam?"

"I fear my husband's weakness and foolishness have become so evident to even the moderate barons that Hiram has no support left in his council. He is irrelevant. The fate of Eswy lies in possession of Eleanor."

She spoke as though I were the crown itself, a trinket of gold and rubies, to be snatched for.

"I made no arrangements for wagons, madam. I beg your pardon. I thought we were leaving by sea."

"Make them then. The sooner we can leave, the better. And send me two couriers, trusted men. One is to wear my livery and ride to Baron Sawfield. He is at the palace with my husband, I believe. The other is to dress as a simple traveler. See he is well provided with all he needs. He will take ship to Hallasbourg secretly and seek an audience with my brother."

"The second letter, madam?" Dame Hestor was curious. So was I. My curiosity lacked the outrage or fear I should have felt, if I had been in my right and sober mind. "You do not truly mean to let Sawfield have her?"

"We have talked of a marriage between Eleanor and her cousin Leopold, to ensure she continues to belong to a good Penitent household. Now it is more important than ever. Through Eleanor's marriage to Leopold, Eswy will come under the crown of Hallaland and we will begin to do the will of Huvehla and take a stand against the warlocks in the north. Does the perverted fool in Dunmorra not see that now he has let the Nightwalkers out of Talverdin, they will not be content until they have taken the whole island again? They need human babies for their sacrifices and fell rites. The more of us they can enslave, the more powerful they will grow." My mother's voice rose, growing shrill. Her fear was real. Lovell would have laughed at it, deriding her as more superstitious than the most ill-educated peasant. He had met Nightwalkers in Cragroyal; he had even met the warlock prince, King Dugald's brother.

But wait, what had my mother said earlier? Marriage? *Leopold*? The shock tried to push the muddle of the drug out of my mind. My cousin Leopold, the crown prince of Hallaland, was a child of nine. And my *cousin*. Peasants knew better than to marry their cousins. The Powers forbade it. And peasants knew what happened when you bred within the same herd of beasts, with no new blood. Lovell had told me. It concentrated weakness, like distilling poison.

"We will withdraw to Narmor. My brother will send a ship, sailing around the south of Eswiland, and a boat will come up the Narra River. It means traveling through the Westwood, but the Narra Valley is supposed to be quite safe, so long as one stays on the river. There are villages all along it. Eleanor will be taken off and be on her way to Hallaland before Sawfield knows she is gone. Neither he nor the warlock-loving king in Dunmorra will have her."

"The man who goes to Hallasbourg should be someone His Grace, your brother, knows," Dame Hestor said, as I turned and climbed the stairs, helping myself with my hands because of the shaking of my knees.

I was cold, and the heat of Katerina in the bed could not warm me.

For the rest of the night, I dreamed of being buried alive.

My father came to see me the next day, while the castle was a swarming anthill of preparation. The gates were closed against him and my mother's men would not open them. Katerina and I watched from the roof of the Old Keep.

A troop of men-at-arms in the yellow and black of Baron Sawfield rode out from the city to join the king. The baron himself led them. He and the king talked. I thought my father looked defeated, slumped in his saddle. He rode away among the baron's men like a captive, his own knights and men-at-arms trailing behind.

I felt abandoned.

CHAPTER THREE
KORBY: MASTER ARVOL AND A ROYAL COMMAND

Master Arvol's room, at the top of a narrow house beside a tavern, smelt of sulphurous sea-coal and bedding that had been too many months without an airing. It reeked of the bitter anger of a man whose thoughts were all of revenge and hatred and the wrongs done him by an unjust world. I stubbed my toe on a table leg, stifling a curse, but the man in the bed slept on, snoring in that heavy way that fat men have.

Enough of this, Maurey had said, once he'd fought off the fever and was on his feet, pale—well, he's always pale—but on the mend. The arm healed slowly, though, and he would carry the scar, like a ridge of melted wax, all swirls and knots of flesh, for life. We needed to know just what Master Arvol was researching. We had to see his notes. We knew he was reading old books and documents related to travel, histories of the conquest of Eswiland, encoded texts of the philosophers' secret arts and works on religious societies in Rona, as well as books on the Nightwalkers. It was worrying, but not enough to tell us what to worry about.

Our invasion of Arvol's room grew more urgent when, lounging around the man's favorite tavern, I heard him announcing he had quit his job. He was going to make a journey down the old highway to Rona, which they said was the greatest city in the world. It was certainly the largest that I knew of. I was not exactly looking forward to following Arvol there; I don't like crowds of people. Their feelings beat on me like madness.

A sudden journey to Rona suggested that something had changed. Arvol had discovered something, found what he was looking for, or been warned by the survivors of the fight in the library to get out. Before we went trailing off to the empire after him, we needed more information, so we didn't walk into another ambush.

Time to read the notes. If we could find them in this mess.

A hand touched my arm. There hadn't been anyone there a moment before. Maurey stood beside me, holding out a candle in a pewter stand.

He couldn't read in the dark. Well, neither could I, but I couldn't see in the dark either, and he could. Nightwalker dark sight showed the world all in strange, muted colors, he said, colors governed by the nature of the objects, but the contrast between ink and parchment or paper was usually too slight for reading.

We didn't need to speak. I snapped my fingers over the wick and the candle lit.

I wasn't just another hired sword, in case that hasn't been made clear yet. Even Maurey, who is the strongest Nightwalker warlock born in generations (and only half a Nightwalker at that), can't light a candle without speaking a spell.

Arvol grunted. I kept my body between the light and the bed. Given the amount of ale he'd drunk with his supper, celebrating the fact he was moving on to better things in Rona, or so he told half the tavern, I doubted we'd have woken him if we'd come singing in the door. In a moment he was snoring again.

We set the candle back on the one small table and moved swiftly around the room, looking through the piles of books stacked on the floor—most stolen from the library. One or two were new, from a press down in Rona, though these were largely

Ronish translations of ancient works. However, most were old, bound in cracked leather, the sort that creak stiffly as you turn handwritten vellum. Some might have been older than Hallow's conquest of Eswiland and the founding of the human kingdom that had eventually split into Dunmorra and Eswy. I couldn't make head or tail of the script when I opened one to look.

Maurey shook his head over them. He's a scholar at heart and to him, stealing from a university library was probably nearly as criminal as treason.

I swear he saw me thinking that. He grinned. Not fair. I'm the one who reads minds, though that isn't a good way to put it. What I do is more like reading hearts, and I often wish I didn't. Living in a roar of other people's emotions isn't something any sane person would choose. Walk the streets in my head and you'll feel the world is full of Arvols.

I felt the prince's surge of excitement run through my own veins when he found what we were looking for. We met at the table, almost knocking our heads together as we leaned to the light of the candle.

Arvol's notes were a thick stack of what I think they call quires, groups of pages laid on one another and then folded over—it was like a book, not yet sewn and bound. It was all held together with a bit of grubby string which I untied with care.

The pages of fine Ronish paper were written in a mixture of ink and lead pencil. Some pages were passages copied from other works. Some were written in code: nonsense and numbers and symbols. Maurey frowned over it.

This was no brief note or list that we could copy out, hiding from Arvol that we'd ever read it. We had to steal the booklet, which would let him know he was being watched.

Was it worth it? Would it make him more careful, harder to follow?

Maurey turned a page and we both stared at a single diagram.

The series of concentric circles took up the whole spread, left and right. Each circle was joined to the next by a single dark line placed seemingly at random around the circuit. It all appeared very carefully drawn. Below it was written: *Symbol of the Yehillon*.

We both recognized it.

"The medal," I whispered. "What's the Yehillon?"

Maurey shook his head. "I've never come across the word before. A family badge? A religious symbol? Different nations do honor different Lesser Powers, but I know I've never heard that name."

Master Arvol groaned, belched and sat up.

"Whazz...?" he said. "Hey!" And then he shouted, "Thieves!", scrambling to get out of bed and grope beneath it for his chamber pot at the same time. As weapons went, that was fighting dirty. Lucky for us he tangled himself in blankets and fell, struggling and cursing.

Maurey thrust the notes down the front of his doublet and grabbed a huge volume from one of the stacks on the floor. It might have looked a random choice, but I doubted it was. He shoved it at me. Master Arvol unrolled himself and stumbled towards us. I didn't draw my sword: hardly the time or place. I just pinched out the candle, and Maurey grabbed my free arm. Arvol hurled the contents of the chamber pot at us.

We weren't there.

"Thieves! Murder! *Nightwalkers!*" shrieked Master Arvol, and his real and honest terror rolled over me in waves.

Actually, we were still there, but in the halfworld, that shadowy, colorless layer of existence into which Nightwalkers like Maurey can step, using darkness as their doorway.

Still gripping my arm, Maurey tugged me towards the open window. Arvol had begun furiously uncorking jars of alchemical ingredients and sniffing them. I don't know what he was searching for, and Maurey obviously didn't want to find out. He scrambled through the window, never letting go of me. I heaved myself through after him, awkward, with the book still under my arm. The hilt of my sword caught on the windowframe. Maurey seemed to shimmer a moment and the world went even mistier. I tumbled down onto the slates of the tavern next door, the lumber of the windowframe suddenly less real than I was.

"I didn't know you could do that," I said.

"Do what?" Maurey asked, leading the way along the ridgepole.

"Go further in the halfworld that way. I thought it was just one layer, or whatever."

"So do most people," he admitted, by which he meant, most Nightwalkers. "But I've found it's even possible to reach a place where you can walk through stone."

"Useful."

"It's not easy," he said, looking back at me. "And it's not an easy place to hold onto. Imagine starting to slip back halfway through a wall."

It's difficult to run along a ridgepole holding on to another person. I lost my balance and my foot slid. Maurey winced at the sudden weight on his bandaged arm and let me go. I took a deep breath, back in the solid, human world, blinking to let my weak, human, night vision return. The prince faded into sight ahead of me.

"Murder! Thieves!" Arvol flung something out the window at us. It fell short, splattering an oily fire over the slates. Arvol screeched and ducked back out of sight when I turned and reached for a throwing-knife. Not that I meant to do more than scare him, no matter what the prince might have thought. We needed him alive if we were going to learn what he was up to and who his allies were.

"Idiot! Don't let him see your face!"

I followed Maurey again. Arvol fell silent. This was not a good time for a Dunmorran foreigner like him to draw attention to himself by waking the neighbors, shouting about Nightwalkers. On much of the continent, particularly in the north, the rare Nightwalker visitor meets with polite interest. But Hallaland is almost as bad as Eswy in its hatred and fear, and everyone who felt that way knew it was the heretic king of Dunmorra who had let the evil Nightwalkers emerge from their hidden kingdom once more.

We scrambled down the roof, knocking tiles loose, hung from the eaves to get a toehold on the lintel of a side door and dropped into the dirty alley. Maurey hauled me into the halfworld again, now that there was no chance of us both falling off the roof, and we ran, his hand on my shoulder, through rotting rubbish that didn't touch us, out to the street and along its mucky length. We stayed in the halfworld all the way back to the house of Sir Dandie, the Dunmorran ambassador to the Hallalandish court. The place was surrounded by a high brick wall, but the porter let us through the gate at a word and the watchdog trotted over, silent and tail-wagging, to welcome us home.

We patted the beast and headed for the front door. Someone had evidently been keeping a lookout; it opened before we could knock.

"Your Highness. Lord Moss'avver." Sir Dandie's secretary bowed to each of us. His tension scratched over my nerves like tiny claws.

"What's happened now?" I groaned. It was only a few hours before dawn, I'd had no sleep the night before either, out skulking around the university again, and I wanted my bed.

"News has come from Eswy, sir," the secretary answered. "The crown prince has died."

"Lovell's dead?" Maurey sounded shocked. I had been up in the Fens among my own people when Prince Lovell visited

Dugald's court in Cragroyal, but Maurey had gotten to know the boy quite well.

"When?" Maurey asked. "And how?"

"The ship carrying the news had a swift crossing from Rensey. Only five days ago. He died at Rensey Palace, at his father's court—an accident of some kind."

"What kind?" I wondered, rubbing the back of my neck. I was starting to get the sort of headache I've learned to fear. White light crawled around the edges of my sight and I had that feverish feeling of the world slowing down around me. For some reason, spending very long in the halfworld often brought such a headache on. It would go away if I ignored it—I hoped. Some Fenlander witches seek visions and welcome them when they come. I'm not one of them.

"Sir Dandie's in the Green Parlor," the secretary prompted. "Your Highness, Lord Moss'avver."

"He doesn't need me," I said.

Maurey gave me one look and nodded. "Get some rest, Korby." He handed me Arvol's notes before heading off with the secretary. "And put those someplace safe with the book, would you?"

I glanced at the volume I'd been carrying: *Cuin's Life of Blessed Miron*, written in Old Ronish, a language I could barely recognize, in a square fading script. Master Miron had been the chief of King Hallow's philosophers, an alchemist and one-time Archmagister of the College of Astrologers in Rona, the man who'd invented the philosopher's fire that burned Nightwalkers but left humans unharmed. There were dozens of tales of his life, but I'd never heard of Cuin. A rare book? I stashed it and the bundle of notes in Maurey's room before returning to my own to wash in a basin of cold water and fall into bed.

Not into sleep, though. My thoughts couldn't seem to slow down. The symbol of the Yehillon. What was the Yehillon? Not a person. But it might be. I'm the Moss'avver, after all, clan chief of the Moss'avvers of the Fens. There's no Clan Yehillon in the Fens, but that didn't mean there wasn't some other land where a chieftain's title was his name, without any nonsense of barons and counts, earls and princes. The crown prince of Eswy was dead and Dugald's bride was heir to the throne. But what did that all mean? King Hiram's council had not liked the betrothal. If they broke it now, who would really be ruling in Eswy? Arvol stole books on old religious groups...*A man stood at the top the stairs...*

The prince woke me an hour later.

"Is it an emergency?" I groaned. My head throbbed.

"Dugald thinks it is. He wants to talk to you too."

"Oh, joy. Does he know something we don't about the prince's death?" Stairs...Why was I seeing stairs?

"Apparently the queen packed up her immediate household, including the princess, who's said to be ill or overcome with grief, and set out for Narmor Castle in the west within a few days of the prince's death. Or planned to—they hadn't left yet when King Hiram sent the courier with his message to Dugald, but they'll be gone by now."

I considered that. Queen Elinda had her own household at Rensey Oldcastle, and everyone knew she and the king hated one another. Was this a long-laid plan, or panic? Had the princess wanted to flee? Her brother had written to Dugald that she was eager for the marriage, but who really knew? Dunmorra was a scary place these days, if you'd been brought up believing Nightwalkers were the monsters in every shadow, going to get you if you were a naughty little child.

I followed Maurey back to his room, where the speaking stone he had made sat on the table, a candle burning to either side. It looked like a boring gray rock the size of a goose egg, split in half, except that inside it was hollow and lined with crystals of amethyst. The king kept the other half. You didn't have to be a warlock to use it; all you needed was the key, the right set of words.

Right now it was activated, the crystals glowing faintly.

"We're back," Maurey said.

"Moss'avver?" King Dugald's voice was quiet but clear, carried by the stone.

"Yes, Your Grace?"

"What do you think?"

"I wonder, why Narmor Castle, sir? So far in the west— the queen's strength comes from here in Hallaland, where her brother rules. Why run the exact opposite way?"

"Narmor is a fortress that's never been taken by siege," Maurey pointed out.

"Bookworm," I muttered, feeling not so clever now. "But who is she going to hold it against? Her husband?"

Dugald laughed, but he didn't sound happy.

"A fast courier arrived here four days after the death of Lovell, Geneh keep him," he said. "A secret courier, with a message from King Hiram. I've been…thinking about it. Discussing it with the council. I wanted to hear what you two thought as well."

"What was the message?" Maurey asked.

"Hiram invited me to come south with an army, for a midsummer wedding."

"Funny thing to do the moment your son dies," I said. Eleanor was supposed to travel north to Cragroyal for a wedding at the autumn equinox in Aramin-month. "Invite the neighbors to invade. What's he afraid of that he thinks you can prevent?"

"A wedding with an army is usually called a war," Maurey said.

The king seemed to agree. "Leaving aside the problem of raising an army in such a short time—that wouldn't be practical anyhow, not by midsummer. But our council certainly doesn't like the idea. It looks as if Hiram is trying to use Dunmorra as a weapon against his own enemies."

"His wife and her brother?" Maurey wondered. "Or his barons?"

"It looks to me like he's practically offering you his crown," I said.

"Yes," said Dugald. "That was part of the message."

Maurey and I were both shocked. "He put that *in writing*?"

"An offer to abdicate in my favor as Eleanor's husband, yes."

"We'll end up with the whole island at war."

"That's what I'm afraid of," Dugald said. "And..." He hesitated. "I'm worried about the princess." He cleared his throat. I could almost see him, sitting a bit hunched before his half of the speaking-stone, twisting his hands together the way he did when he was nervous. "If you think this is the wrong thing to do, say so. Tell me I'm being foolish. But...I'd like you two to leave Arvol for now. Sir Dandie can have someone else follow him to Rona. I want...I'd like you two to go after Eleanor."

"And?" Maurey asked.

"Offer help if she needs help. Bring her north to Dunmorra, if that's what she wants, but take her up to Greyrock rather than Cragroyal."

"Why, sir?" I asked. Greyrock Town is a shabby little frontier town crouched beneath a big dark castle, not exactly Dunmorra at its best.

"I'm going to be heading to Greyrock Town myself in a few days. Queen Ancrena and I are meeting to discuss the appointment of the new Warden of Greyrock."

Right, the old warden, never happy about Nightwalkers actually being allowed to come through the pass from Talverdin that Greyrock Castle guarded, had resigned his post the previous autumn, retiring to his manor in the east. Dugald and the

Talverdine ambassador had been talking about having a mixed garrison of humans and Nightwalkers there, an experiment in living together.

"The meeting's too important to cancel," Dugald went on. "No Nightwalker ruler has left the protection of Talverdin since Hallow's day, so this shows incredible trust on her part."

"I know."

"Could you leave your half of the speaking-stone for my ambassador in Rensey and teach him how to activate it? Things could change quite quickly in Eswy, and if they do, I want to know about it."

"Of course. But what if the princess doesn't want to go to Dunmorra?" Maurey asked.

"Escort her back to her father in Rensey. It must be her will to come to Dunmorra, not ours, no matter how much safer we think she'd be. I—I think she, er, I think she favors the match..." Poor Dugald. He was in love with a woman he'd never seen; he was in love with a few secret letters, a sketch done by her brother and a piece of music. I have to admit, the music stirred *my* heart, and if it really had been she who had written it, and written it especially for him..."But I won't marry any woman who isn't willing."

Yes, the mother of Dugald and Maurey had been married against her will, and that had led to tragedy. The peace that Maurey and Dugald had made out of that tragedy was a fragile thing, and they would both destroy their own lives, trying to preserve it.

Which is why they, and all Dunmorra and Talverdin, needed people like me to look after it and them.

"We need to keep the peace in all this. Somehow. I won't march over the border just because King Hiram thinks his barons are plotting against him. Not without more certain evidence that Dunmorra is threatened. But I won't have Eswy stirred up into a holy war against us and Talverdin, which is what Hiram's opponents want."

"That may be what Arvol wants too," Maurey suggested. "Are you sure you want to pull us off him? I have his notes to decipher. They might be important."

"Korby?" Dugald asked, pleading and informal. "Have you *seen* anything related to this? Any sign what I should do? Or will you try to see, for me?"

I shook my head, forgetting he was several hundred miles away and that the stone did not carry sight. I wasn't absolutely refusing his request, but I hoped it wasn't an order. Vision— past, future, might-have-beens—should come easily, if I tried. The white-edged headache still pressed on me. I hadn't slept long enough to leave it behind. The truth was, I did not want to try. I feared my visions. Too often they showed me only death that I was already too late to prevent. Though if there had been any truth in my dreams...I had seen something already. Maurey elbowed me. What had I been going to tell Dugald? Something about Rensey Palace? No. It was Narmor we were talking about.

"But...if the princess disappears into Narmor Castle, and it's as impregnable as Maurey says, she may never come out. *They pushed the prince down the stairs.*"

"Who?" Maurey demanded.

And Dugald asked, "You've heard something?"

"What?" I heard my own speech, very far away and slurred, the headache exploding, white spears of light jabbing my temples. I took a deep breath, hands over my eyes.

"You said, 'They pushed the prince down the stairs," Maurey prompted.

I looked up at him. He seemed hazy, colorless and shimmering, as though I were seeing an echo of the halfworld.

A young man, my age maybe, thinner though, and shorter,

silhouetted against light from a narrow window. He looks back over his shoulder, hearing something. Dark shape, dark gown, like a master's robe. A sudden swing, no time to duck, to cry out—a cudgel had been hidden in the wide sleeve. He arches forward like a diver, down the stone stairs, but I think he is already dying...

"...already dying, already dead!" The voice in my ears was my own.

Maurey shook me. I shivered and muttered, "Powers! What was that? What did I say?"

"Murder," said Dugald, who had heard every word. He sounded shaken.

"Sorry, Your Grace," I muttered. The Yerku help me, I was a warrior, not a toothless grandfather, mad and mumbling fortunes to beg for his bread in the marketplace, though I've known Fenlander witches come to that. Vision was something that should creep up on you in decent privacy, like illness, not lay you bare before the world. I couldn't stop shaking. Maurey put an arm over my shoulders.

"Would you recognize the assassin?"

I shut my eyes: a shape in a black robe. "Not to see him, not to swear to his face at a trial. But the feel of his mind—I would know it again. He enjoyed that, found it exciting." It made me ill, touching even in vision a mind of that shape, that flavor. The stink of a long-dead carcass—think of that. I coughed, trying not to gag, recalling it. "He's someone rotten with envy, wanting what the prince had—power, admiration. Hating him for having it and wasting it. It's hard to put into words; they just aren't enough. But I'd know him again, sure as if I'd seen his face."

"Lord Moss'avver, I'm sending you to protect the princess," Dugald said. Royal command, that was, and I knew better than to argue. The king had a stubborn streak, and once you hit it, nothing further you could do would budge him. "Maurey...?"

He couldn't command his half-brother, who was a prince of Talverdin, not of Dunmorra. But in that word was all his faith: *I trust you. Help me.*

"Yes," Maurey said simply. "We'll leave at dawn. Korby needs to sleep."

Korby was going to throw up. Visions do that to me anyway, even when they aren't so filthy. It's not an uncommon reaction, but Powers, I hated the shaming weakness of it. I started to lurch to my feet, but Maurey, who'd seen me come out of visions a time or two in the past, pulled me back, put a hand that felt like it was burning on the back of my neck and murmured in Talverdine. The pounding headache lessened and the uncontrollable shuddering stopped.

"Useful spell, that, warlock," I muttered, a bit short of breath, but feeling infinitely better.

"Beats your cures any day, witch," Maurey agreed, having smelled the tea I brewed when a bad vision hit like a hangover.

"Any messages for Annot, Maurey?" Dugald asked. "She's coming down from Oakhold to travel to Greyrock with me."

"Give her my love. And don't worry. We'll keep your princess safe, whatever comes."

Maurey touched the stone, spoke a line of Talverdine verse, and the light faded. It was just a pretty paperweight.

We looked at one another, both a bit gray, though it showed up worse on Maurey, whose milk-white skin, never human pink or brown, was a stark contrast to his coal-black eyes and hair, displaying every bruise and weary shadow. The tales that tell you magic is without cost are children's stories, nothing more.

"You know," I pointed out, "hiding here or sailing on a ship crewed by the king's men, that's one thing. Riding across Eswy is something else entirely, and you can't count on it being dark enough to slip into the halfworld every time we see someone coming. Not only do we have to pack, we have to change the color of your skin. You're going to have to use that alchemical dye your friend Romner invented."

Maurey made a face.

"And," I said mercilessly, "you'll have to cut your hair."

I knew I'd lost that argument before it began. Maurey didn't fight fair. "I'll cut mine if you cut yours," he said, with a nasty smile. Nightwalkers wear their hair at least to their shoulders, but no Fenlander man cuts his hair at all. If you didn't have braids, you'd just be a big scruffy Dunmorran, right?

"Anyway," he said, "if I'm dark enough, I can be a Dravidaran and hide my hair under a turban."

"You don't speak Dravidaran."

"Who does, in this part of the world? Jumble together Ronish and Hallish and Eswyn with a Dunmorran accent and who can tell what kind of foreigner I am?" He grinned. "Or I could put my hair in pigtails and cover myself in mud and burrs and say I'm a dark Fenlander."

"You don't have the noble bearing and dignity to carry it off."

"I don't smell like a damp sheep, you mean."

I mimed a punch.

In the end, we went with the Dravidaran plan. A Dravidaran traveler was strange and exotic, but not impossible, and nobody burned Dravidarans, so far as we knew. We crossed the narrow Eswyn Sea on a fast smack owned by Dugald and crewed by his men, the same one that had brought us here, sailing up the River Esta to put in at Rensey Harbor after a voyage of only four days. Perhaps Maurey and I between us had wished up a rare good wind from the east. That was just enough time for the king to have sent my horses down from Cragroyal; we might have been able to travel faster with Maurey's swift white Talverdines, but they'd have been rather noticeable in Eswy.

Rensey was a city on edge. The king had not been seen since shortly after his son's death, and the black and yellow liveried men of the Baron of Sawfield were everywhere. No one seemed to know where the baron himself was. Some said the palace; some said he had returned to his estates on the south coast, leaving his nephew Lord Gillem "in attendance" on the king; others said that he had taken a troop of his men-at-arms and ridden west. We didn't have time to track down the rumors; we stayed only long enough to make sure the horses were rested and sound after their hasty journey from Cragroyal, before following the queen and princess west to Narmor.

☩ Chapter Four ☩
Eleanor: On the Road to Narmor

Narmor Castle lay almost three hundred miles west of the city of Rensey. My father, in his regular circuit around the kingdom, usually passed the autumn there. My mother's household went in the heat of Melkinas, to avoid the stench that drifted over Rensey Oldcastle from the harbor. I had never before been to Narmor in the spring.

The several days of preparation and the first days of our journey afterwards passed as though in a dream. I seemed to feel nothing. The discussion between my mother and Dame Hestor that I had overheard might as well have been years in the past, for all I thought of it. People say "numb with grief"; it is a true description. I went through the days like a puppet obedient to my strings: rising, eating, riding, praying, as I was told. Sometimes I broke into tears for no apparent reason: the sight of a meadowlark swaying on a wild rose cane, pouring out its heart in song; rain; a harsh word from my mother. I had not even thought to ask Katerina to be sure the little chest containing my flutes and books found its way into our baggage. The music in my heart had dried up. The wordless song that had shaped itself in my poppy-addled mind the night Lovell died was forgotten.

Only when I heard riders behind us did an ember of emotion begin to burn. Some part of me was waiting for my father's knights to overtake us and demand my return. The terms of my unhappy parents' marriage treaty gave Lovell's upbringing to my father and mine to my mother. Now that I was the heir, surely I belonged to my father.

But no knights in the royal red and gold ever appeared. Two days out from Rensey, a courier came from Baron Sawfield with a letter for my mother. Her lips thinned when she read it. "The baron writes that he will come to Narmor for the Midsummer Feast," she told her ladies, "and afterwards, he will escort Her Highness the Crown Princess back to her father in Rensey."

"We do not keep such feasts, sirrah," she informed the courier. "They are merely an excuse for gluttony, drunkenness and wanton behaviour. But the baron will be welcome, of course, to join us in our prayers, as on any day."

An answer that was no answer.

The courier bowed. She gave him no written reply. I noticed that Katerina managed to talk privately with the rider for a few moments before he left.

"I thought your father might have sent you some word by him," she explained.

"Did he?" I asked.

"No."

"Ah."

"The man did tell me that Sawfield has offered the king his protection," she said.

Protection from what? That was what Lovell would have asked. Was Sawfield not someone my father needed protection *from*? But I could not be Lovell, and I said nothing.

After that courier, we left the wagons to follow at their own pace and rode, if not like couriers ourselves—a mounted man, without changes of horse, can ride from Rensey to Narmor Castle in a week if the roads are good—at least with haste indecent for a royal procession, only a few packhorses carrying our essentials.

Even so, I doubt we covered much more distance in a day than a person afoot would have; we usually traveled at a walk, stopping for long midday meals and periods of prayer and meditation at the set hours. Despite that, my body, not used to riding, ached with the long days and the jolting gait of my mount. I had sores in unspeakable places, other sores on my lower thighs, almost as unspeakable, from the horns of the sidesaddle. Each night we slept at another manor house. Some were royal manors, some belonged to barons or mere knights. Each night I lay drifting in and out of tormented dreams I could never remember. Katerina, beside me, always seemed to sleep with the soundness of an untroubled mind. When it was a small manor, one or two of my mother's ladies would share the bed as well. Too many of them snored.

One night, almost two weeks after we had left Rensey, I could stand it no longer. I rose, pulled on my boots, wrapped myself in a shawl and crept through the house. No one saw me. A serving-boy slept on a bench near the door, but he did not stir as I lifted the heavy bar and slipped outside. The manor was unfortified, little more than a glorified farmstead. A rutted lane wound through outbuildings. Somewhere a cow lowed and an owl hooted as if in answer.

I left the lane, climbed a stile over a hedge and found myself walking on grazed turf, short and springy to the feet. Thoughts of Nightwalkers or damned and wandering shades never crossed my mind, not with any real fear. I knew I should be afraid, but I was not. I did not even feel any worry about meeting a bull, which Lovell would have warned me was a more sensible fear. The air was sweet with honeysuckle.

I stretched, as if I were waking up, and my feet found the rut of a cow-path. It climbed a low hill, and I followed.

I had never in my life been outside four walls at night. Even when Katerina and I crept away to the Old Keep, we were still safe inside the great curtain-wall of Rensey Oldcastle. Here, I was alone, and free. I thought of the Rose Maiden's most popular song, in which the starling laments that it must sing in a cage, making music out of memory of sun and sky. In the end, the starling dies, its heart breaking.

I had thought it very beautiful and sad, but now it seemed a horrible song. Why did the bird not seize its chance and swoop out? Someone must have opened the door to feed it, after all. Why did it not try to fly? What was the Rose Maiden thinking of, to write such a verse?

But she had written another song. It was not so popular, because it told a story from Rossmark in the far north, and such barbarian tales were not fashionable. The princess in that song sets off to find the home of the North Wind, who has imprisoned her lover.

Seven seas I'll sail upon
Seven winters long
Seven mountains climb upon
Through seven summers gone...

And the repeated burden, the chorus, of the song is this:

But never doubt I'll come to you
Though cold death stands between.

That was a better song, though the tune was not so fine. The woman in that song never gave up. I had been giving up.

I looked up at the stars and the fat silver disc of the moon, and my heart began to race. It was an excitement almost like fear. I would be the starling no longer. I would be instead the princess seeking the home of the North Wind. I would be the Rose Maiden herself, who, so the stories in Rensey said, was a noblewoman who had fled betrothal to a tyrant to live a minstrel's life dedicated to the Great Power Ayas the Smith, patron of artists. Other stories said she was the prince's peasant mistress, or a Ronish Sister of Mayn, or a mystic who saw visions like the barbarian witches of the far north, but I liked the story of the Rose Maiden who fled the tyrant and wandered the world, hiding her beauty under a tattered veil, only her music revealing her true self. That Rose Maiden would not ride along like a living shade. That Rose Maiden would rebel. She would disdain excuses and the weak traitor thoughts that said I should be obedient, safe and—mindless. Lovell had given me music. He had given me books. He had, most of all, taught me that I belonged to myself, and that my mind was free. I would not betray him. I would not betray myself.

I would not betray my kingdom, but I did just that if I let my mother make me a puppet queen under the control of Hallaland and the joyless Penitent beliefs of its royal house. Lovell had told me how peasants were whipped for dancing and singing on feastdays in my uncle's kingdom. Lovell said that to teach that joy was a sin was merely a means of controlling others by enslaving their minds and reducing them to captive beasts. Classes at Hallasbourg University had been nearly shut down, allowed to teach only what the Penitents approved, and some of the masters were imprisoned or driven into exile. Lovell believed the Powers intended human intelligence to question and explore the world and build knowledge upon knowledge. Did I want that for Eswy?

What would the Rose Maiden choose?

Baron Sawfield was no Penitent, but he was a brute who hanged a peasant for startling his horse. Shipwrecked Nightwalker captives had died in Sawfield's prison, back before I was born. Murdered, executed, suicides…the stories varied, but he had certainly planned to burn them alive in philosopher's fire. I had heard him boast of it, when I had been grudgingly allowed by my mother to attend the midwinter feast at Rensey Palace. The baron had been talking of the corruption of Eswy that would follow my marriage to Dugald of Dunmorra, as though Nightwalkers would immediately swarm over the land, ravaging it. *He* knew how to deal with warlocks, he said...

Come to think of it, that was the very day Lovell had given me the first of the secret letters from King Dugald, the one that called me "Dearest lady" and praised the beauty of the piece of music I had given Lovell to send to him.

As for Sawfield...his courier had claimed to Katerina that the king was "under his protection."

My father was his captive, as those long-dead Nightwalkers had been.

In a ballad I would simply ride into the nearest market town and proclaim myself, and knights would swarm to follow me. We would ride on Rensey, the countryside rising to join my army, Baron Sawfield would surrender on bended knee... The Rose Maiden might write a song about such a tale.

I could hear Lovell laughing.

One thing in that silly thought was true. On my own I was weak. I needed an army to save my father and keep my kingdom.

The owl soared somewhere overhead, calling again. It was heading west.

In a ballad, there should have been a sign. The Rose Maiden would have made certain to include one. I drew a long breath, my mind made up. Lovell had not believed that the Great Powers or the Lesser sent signs. "We have minds," he would say. "We have reason. We're supposed to use them."

But I would go west, like the owl.

I remembered reading descriptions of our island. Narmor lay almost under the eaves of the Westwood.

The Westwood reached into only the northwestern corner of Eswy, but it covered over a quarter of Dunmorra and stretched almost to Cragroyal.

I would go to King Dugald, but not by way of the highways and the guarded bridges over the River Esta. I could not go yet, though. I could not run away in my nightgown. Besides, if I fled on the open road, they would find me in hours. I needed to be close enough to the Westwood to reach it in one journey. From what I remembered of previous trips, we were nearly there. Perhaps tomorrow, I told myself. Yes, tomorrow night I would be prepared.

I headed back towards the house. For the first time in days, I seemed to be alive again, though being alive meant that there was an ache, a terrible emptiness in my heart. I had not imagined it was possible to feel so, and get up and go on, but people did. They had to.

"Your Highness?"

A pale shape floated forward from the darkness of the hedge. I shrieked and jumped back. The ghostly shape spoke.

"Eleanor?"

"Katerina?" I rubbed a hand over my face, laughing weakly. "I thought you were…" I did not finish the sentence. A Nightwalker come to cut my throat? The shade of my brother? I did not know. "What are you doing here?"

"What am I doing here?" She closed the gap between us and seized my hands. "What are *you* doing here? Wandering around alone in your nightgown."

"I've been thinking," I said.

"What about?"

"What's that?" I stepped back hastily. Something Katerina was holding had brushed against me.

"What?" She raised her hand. I stared at the heavy dagger, long as her forearm. "This? For protection. In case…Well, I woke up and you were gone, Eleanor. The night-candle was still there, so I knew you hadn't gone out to the"—she made a ladylike pause—"the, um, little house. And anyway, there was the chamber pot. I looked, and you weren't anywhere in the house. I was afraid for you. You shouldn't go out into the night. It's dangerous."

"You didn't wake anyone!" I exclaimed.

"I'm not a fool! I should have, though. You've been acting so strangely lately. I…I thought of the duckpond. But then I saw something moving in the lane, so I followed. I lost you when you went over the hedge, and the field is so dark…there could have been anything in it."

"So instead of coming to rescue me, you waited. Where did you get that dagger, anyway?"

"Don't make fun of me, Your Highness." She pulled her shawl more closely about her body, as if to hide beneath it from the darkness. I noticed she did not answer my question. "We're getting close to the Westwood, you know, and they say Nightwalkers travel through it to Cragroyal all the time. It's an evil place."

This was probably not the moment to tell her what I had decided.

"Come back to bed," she said, taking my arm. "Before… before something sees us out here."

"There's no one to see."

But I went with her to the stile and walked arm in arm with her back to the house. She was shivering.

"Thank you," I whispered, when we were nearly at the door. "Thank you for not waking anyone. I just needed some time alone to…to pray in private."

Katerina gave my arm an understanding squeeze.

The boy still slept on his bench. We barred the door again and made it back to bed undetected. The night-candle still burned in its glass shield. Katerina sheathed the dagger and rolled it up in the bundle of stockings she was knitting.

In the morning neither of us mentioned my midnight stroll.

Chapter Five
Eleanor: Escape

The evening of the day following my great decision, I discovered a flaw in my plan.

Narmor Castle was nearly in sight. Master Sneyth rode back to tell the ladies surrounding Katerina and me that the queen had decided we would not stop, but would press on, arriving at Narmor an hour or two after nightfall, if that was Huvehla's will.

One part of me felt great relief. It was too late to do anything rash. I had missed my chance. Huvehla's will be done.

Starlings were warbling—and cackling, they are not always very musical—as we passed beneath an elm tree.

No.

I must have whispered the word aloud. "What did you say?" Katerina asked, looking over at me. "Your Highness?" she added, as Master Sneyth and several waiting-women and maids also turned.

"No," I whispered. I shut my eyes. I only wanted to prevent myself weeping, to be not the helpless princess but the bold Rose Maiden, but I must have looked pale and upset enough to worry Katerina.

"The princess faints!" she cried, and twitched her horse over, reaching out to me.

Yes, I thought. Now Anaskto, the Lesser Power who anoints and protects kings, help me. I swayed. I looked around wildly. I sagged.

It is actually difficult to fall when your leg is hooked over the upper pommel of a sidesaddle and your horse is only walking, but I did my best. I flopped forwards on the horse's neck, letting the reins slide from my grasp, dropping my whip.

My mount shambled to a stop.

Master Sneyth, again, was there, leaping from his own horse to take me in his arms, while Katerina ordered a man-at-arms to help her down.

After one quick glance through my lashes at Master Sneyth's pinched face and Katerina's worried one, I kept my eyes shut and lay limp in my tutor's arms. He smelled unpleasantly like what he was—one of those Penitents who regarded bathing as pampering the flesh.

"Wretched girl," one of the women said.

Katerina flew to my defence. "How dare you, madam! To be dragged across the country like this in her grief, not even allowed to see her brother decently buried—is it any wonder she's ill?"

"We cannot delay," said Dame Hestor. "The Baron of Sawfield may be—"

"If he were planning to prevent us going to Narmor, he would have overtaken us long before now."

Someone else wailed, "We should never have left the wagons to follow."

"The sooner we are safe within Narmor's walls, the better," I heard my mother say, interrupting the argument. "Can she ride?"

"Another hysterical tantrum?" asked one of the women in the background.

"Poor child's worn out, and no wonder," a man's voice said. One of the grooms, I thought.

"No, Your Grace," said Katerina, answering the queen. She held my hand between both her own. "She can't ride. She's insensible."

"Hot," I muttered, tossing in Master Sneyth's grip, "so hot."

And I squeezed Katerina's hand with my fingers.

I felt her hesitation. I felt as a gambler must feel when he throws the dice with his last farthing at stake. But I did not pray to Huvehla, Power of Chance and Fate, as gamblers did—a very different Huvehla from my mother's, little different from the Lesser Power Sypat, whom the gamblers also invoked.

Anaskto of Holiness, Anaskto of Kingship, please, if I am destined to rule, help me do this, so that I may be a free queen of a free people...

Katerina rubbed my hand. "She's fevered," she declared. "Madam, she must rest. She cannot go on tonight."

"She doesn't feel fevered to me," Master Sneyth said doubtfully. "A trifle warm, perhaps."

Heavy footsteps came up. I flinched when a sudden dampness landed on my face, but it was only Katerina bathing me with a cloth some kind knight had wet from a water flask.

"There, there, poor dear," she murmured.

"The princess suffers from a weak and hysterical nature," rumbled the voice of my mother's physician, and I felt his pudgy fingers take my wrist. My heart raced, but perhaps that was as well. A rapid pulse might convince him I was truly ill. "Wine of poppies will always be—"

"Poppy wine, poppy wine—you'll addle the child's mind, sir!" said Master Sneyth. I had not realized Master Sneyth thought I had a mind. "You'll corrupt her very soul. Huvehla did not mean for us to live as cowards, using the poisonous dreams of the poppy to avoid the hardships she sends. Perhaps if you took less of your own medicine yourself, you would realize the danger—"

"Sirs!" snapped the queen. "Is my daughter fit to ride?"

She did not dismount, did not come to take my wrist.

I moaned.

"No, Your Grace," said the physician. "We must get her to bed as soon as possible. If she falls into another fit of hysteria as she did in Rensey, she may sink into a decline. It would be dangerous to risk it, with the rigours of a sea voyage ahead of her. The weakness of her mind is such that—"

"She is weakened by grief and these long days in the saddle have exhausted her, Your Grace," Master Sneyth said. "A period of meditation on the inscrutable wisdom of Huvehla's will amid the peace and solitude of Narmor will be her best cure. But Master Findley is right, she cannot ride on tonight. If we could find a wagon…"

"Jolting her about in a wagon will do yet more harm," the physician declared.

"These lands are held by a knight of Narmor," my mother said. "His manor lies half a mile to the north. We will take her there."

It was surprisingly easy to stay limp as I was passed to the sergeant of the Hallaland guards—Master Sneyth not being trusted to manage both me and a horse.

It was not a game of dice and chance I was playing. It was chess, where the moving queen was a power and the king was more properly viewed as the crown, the symbol of kingship, to be protected, to be seized. I would not be that symbol. I would be a queen, a disguised queen, only mistaken for a pawn. My first move had succeeded. I gained another night outside the prison of Narmor.

Katerina did not share my bed that night, but slept on a cot usually used by the maidservant of the knight's daughters, whose pleasant chamber with its whitewashed walls we had to ourselves. The knight and his family were in Rensey, attendant on the king, but his steward made us welcome. Most of my mother's women and servants had continued on to Narmor. My mother remained, as had her armed escort. After all, I was the prize any pursuer would be seeking.

My stomach grumbled. Bread sopped in broth is not a satisfying meal if you are not ill. I had made a pretence of forcing myself to eat, propped up languidly on pillows, and had feigned sleep afterwards. At least Master Findley's poppy wine had not been offered again. Katerina had kept busy harassing servants, having certain items of baggage carried up from the stables, even though the queen was determined we would leave first thing in the morning. Katerina had done a great deal of running up and down herself, before going early to bed and to sleep.

Finally the house was still, and I crept from the bed. Katerina's breathing did not change. The window curtains were drawn, shutting out the moonlight. I needed to find my clothes, take food…a prisoner escaping in enemy territory could not choose starvation over stealing. Should I take a horse? No. I would need someone to saddle it, someone to boost me into the saddle. I had never had to tend my own horse; learning how while on the run seemed a bad idea. I would simply disappear, and if Anaskto the Power of Kingship was with me, they would think I had fled back towards Rensey and my father, and search east instead of west. My plan was to flee west into the forest and then to follow the eaves of the Westwood up into Dunmorra and around to the northeast, and so make my stealthy way to Cragroyal.

"Tell me what this is about." Katerina's voice, coming suddenly out of the darkness, made me drop the boot I had just found.

"I…I'm just going…I need to…"

"Another walk in the darkness?"

I said nothing.

"Don't you trust me, Eleanor? I thought we'd become friends."

"You're supposed to be my mother's spy," I mumbled.

"And who warned you of that when we first met? I did. Have I ever betrayed anything important? I tell her the little things. I tell her when you wear flowers in your hair, when you dance or sing visiting your father's court, which she could guess at anyway. I tell her when you don't say your prayers at night. I've never betrayed the things that matter, the true secrets you've trusted me enough to share. I've never told her about your music—and did you even notice that poor Master Sneyth didn't either? Or about when we went swimming in the river, or—"

"This is…this is more than those. I don't want to put you in danger."

Katerina gave an odd laugh. "Danger. Like running around in the night? Here in Eswiland, of all places, and so far west? Do you even understand the danger, or are you like Prince Lovell, sneering at the idea of danger in the darkness because the king of Dunmorra keeps a tame warlock and says, 'Look everyone, they're harmless after all'? Like a man who feeds a lion and thinks that makes it a kitten? If his neighbors decide to believe it's just a mouser, they'll suffer as he does, when it grows bored of humouring him."

"Katerina…"

"Tell me what you're doing. Are you going to run back to Rensey?"

"Yes," I said after a moment.

"Fool. How do you think you'll make it on your own? What do you know about the world? Only what you've read in Lovell's books. You think it's all a song. A woman traveling on her own isn't going to find brave and honorable champions ready to lay down their lives for her, you know. A woman on her own—"

"I'm not a fool," I said, "but I have to risk it."

"The Baron Sawfield's not a fool either," Katerina said. "You don't need to run back to Rensey, Eleanor. He—I'm sure he has an idea what you're mother's planning. He'll be here before midsummer, before they can smuggle you away to Hallaland. Um, from something the courier, er, let drop, I think perhaps the baron is not so far away as we think. Perhaps he, um, suspects your mother's plan and means to prevent you being sent away from Narmor. Just wait. He'll come for you, once he knows that things are settled in Rensey. I'm sure of it."

"Once what things are settled in Rensey?"

She dismissed that with an impatient flick of her hand. "Don't worry so. Your father's under Sawfield's protection, I told you that. There's no need for you to run away, but if you really mean to then I'll—"

"Katerina," I said, sitting down by her on the cot. There was no way to avoid telling the truth. "I—I'm not going to Rensey. They'll look on the roads east first of all. I'm going to Dunmorra."

"To Dunmorra!"

"I'm going into the Westwood, tonight. I can get around the upper reaches of the River Esta that way, so I won't be questioned at the bridges crossing the border. Then I'll head north and east along the edge of the forest. I'll go to Cragroyal, to King Dugald, as my father wants."

"But...you can't!"

"I'm going to."

"You are a fool. Are you planning to beg? Sell your body?"

"Sell?" I asked, puzzled. Then, from things I had overheard the guards talking of, things they would have been punished for saying if my mother knew I had heard, I realized what she meant. I slapped her.

"Forgive me," we both said at once.

"Your Highness," Katerina added, her voice quiet. "But," she went on, "you must realize what men will assume, if you have no other skills to support yourself. Even if you did, no woman would travel alone. Do you have any idea what such a journey will be like?"

"No," I admitted, "but I will endure it. I can sing," I added. "You see? I won't be quite begging. But I wish I'd brought my pipes."

After a moment she said, "I brought your chest with us. I even had it carried up here tonight."

"You did?" I hugged her. "Oh, Katerina, I'm sorry. I should have trusted you. You are my friend, my only friend, I know it. I'm sorry."

She sighed, perhaps because she knew it was joy at having my flutes that made me proclaim such affection. "I knew you'd want them, if we were going to steal away tonight."

"We?"

"You wouldn't get ten miles on your own. But if I come with you...my mother and uncles gave me an education that wasn't all ladylike," she said. "See? I have secrets too. I know how to get across country without being seen. I can help you get to Sawfield—all right, I mean to Rensey, without your mother's people finding you."

"Or to Dunmorra?"

"Eleanor," she whispered, "please, don't ask that."

"Nightwalkers aren't monsters," I said. "Lovell—" I gulped, speaking his name aloud. "Lovell knew the warlock prince and the Nightwalker ambassador. They're people, like us, he said. No different than, than people from Gehtaland or Rossmark in the north or—"

"They aren't," said Katerina. "Even in Rossmark people are human, no matter how strange and heathen their customs. Nightwalkers are...they're *wrong*, an abomination to the Powers, an insult to nature. They aren't human. *They don't belong in this world.*"

"I'm going to Cragroyal," I said. "I'm sorry. I pledged my hand to Dugald. I won't break my word."

"No one will hold you to that contract. Your father forced you against your will."

"Not against my will," I said. "With it, with all my will." And I still could not bring myself to tell her about the secret letters arranged by Lovell, still could not say, "I…I think I…" Love? I had never set eyes on the man. "I think it's the best choice for Eswy," I said.

"Then I'll come with you," Katerina said in a small voice, and she clutched the neck of her gown where her tarnished amulet lay hidden, "into the Westwood and Dunmorra. Someone has to look after you. And the Powers save us both."

Packing was quickly achieved. Katerina lit more candles from the night-light and made a rolled bundle inside a blanket for each of us. She acted as if she knew just what she was doing; she had already planned what to take, what to leave behind. Flint and fire-steel. Changes of linen, warm shawls, stockings, a loaf of dark bread, a suet pudding, meat pastries and a handful of wizened last-fall's apples, as well as a leather bottle of small beer.

"You knew…"

"I knew you were too stubborn for your own good," she muttered. "As soon as you took your little fit on the road there, I knew you were planning something." She looked over at me and grinned. "You know, when your betrothal to the Dunmorran was announced and my mother persuaded my father to send me to his dear childhood friend, your mother, I heard all about you. I thought you were going to be a prim little puppet, holy as Blessed Elinda, the founder herself, and with the backbone of an earthworm. I was quite happy to find you were so much more interesting."

"Interesting?" I asked, not sure if I was being insulted.

"But," Katerina went on, "playing little tunes to make your big brother proud of you isn't quite preparation for taking the fate of the kingdom into your own hands."

With a defiant look, she unrolled the dagger from her knitting and fastened its sheath onto a belt. I thought she wanted me to make some comment that would let her go on reducing me to a helpless child, so I kept silent.

I almost cried with something like relief, though, as I handled my flutes and recorders, the oiled wood silken to my fingers, the silver bands that strengthened the flutes gleaming softly where the candlelight touched them, the ivory of the little descant recorder palely cool. They seemed like friends banished for long months, though it had not been even a fortnight and it was I who had turned my back on them.

I needed to play. I needed to make music. I was not whole unless I could.

Katerina noticed when I took my books and papers out of the chest as well.

"You can't carry books through the forest," she said. "They're heavy. You don't need them."

"They're from Lovell," I protested.

"Leave them."

I bit my lip. Then, reluctantly, I locked them back in the chest and pushed it under the bed. She was right. But I kept my papers, my music, and I took Dugald's letters out of the book on mathematics where they had been hidden even from Katerina, who had no interest in that art. The letters talked of little things, not secrets, but personal, private things—his bluehounds, the palace gardens, music (he played the lute himself). These I did wrap well and add to my bundle with my pipes, when Katerina was not looking. I did not need her saying anything else rude. Just because she moved with the weight of that dagger, almost a short sword, on her hip as though she was used to it…

My bundle still seemed very heavy. And I was going to have to carry it myself. No servants. No packhorse.

The Rose Maiden was not a whiner.

We dressed in our warmest gowns. I left my hair in the two long plaits Katerina had put it in when she helped me into bed. It felt so much easier on my head than the hard little knot that pulled the hair back so painfully from my face. A shawl over hair and shoulders was not the Rose Maiden's mysterious veil, but it would have to do as a disguise. I did not look much like a princess. I never had. I did not look much like a minstrel, either. With another shawl tying the roll of my belongings to my back, I looked more like a hunchback than anything, I suspected.

That did not help me to feel very heroic.

Katerina managed to stand up straight. I did not.

But we made it out of the house without anyone hearing or seeing us, and Katerina, with a knowing glance up at the stars, led the way along winding rutted lanes and footpaths.

She really was afraid. She kept a hand on the hilt of her dagger the whole time and eventually hooked her left arm through mine, almost dragging me along every time my steps slowed.

I did not care. My heart was a bird, flying free. An owl floating into the west. A starling—no, they were rather stubby-winged, unromantic birds in the air—a hawk, released from its jesses. A swallow following the sun. A tune started to shape itself, and the words began to jostle into place.

I was the Rose Maiden, striding into freedom, into the vast mystery of the Westwood where anything could happen. I was escaping to my love…I blushed even thinking that.

I was a silly child whose shoulders were already starting to ache, whose boot was rubbing on her heel, whose stomach rumbled with hunger.

But my heart was still a bird.

I felt less like making songs by the time the sky grew gray with coming dawn. We had walked perhaps a dozen miles and most of them had been a nightmare, a horrible unending dream of one foot after the other.

Dawn found us huddled together between the buttressing feet of an ancient elm. I still had enough spirit, or spite, to notice that Katerina was as exhausted as I was. We ate and drank without speaking and fell asleep without seeking a better place to hide.

But we had reached the daylong green twilight of the Westwood, and its trees were all around us.

My second move, I thought hazily. But against whom was I playing? My mother? Baron Sawfield? Katerina? All of them?

PART TWO

✣ CHAPTER SIX ✣

ELEANOR: DANCING IN THE WESTWOOD

Two days later, the food was nearly gone and what was left was not fit for pigs. My shoulders still ached, my feet were wrapped in rags to ease my blisters, my nose was peeling with sunburn, and I did not care. I was the Rose Maiden, and I was playing a leaping five-step for a village dance in the Westwood.

"You'll be a couple of those Penitent missionaries of the queen's we've heard of," a burly villager had said that afternoon, when the path we were following became a well-traveled muddy track and we limped out into the open between fields of barley and peas and turnips, with a cluster of reed-thatched roofs in the distance.

I had blinked in the sudden bright sun, staring at the handful of people—a family, I guessed, men and women and children from a bent old man down to a child of four or five—who were hoeing the turnip field. They were all sweaty and dirty and not so brightly dressed as the peasants at the village festivals Lovell had taken me to over the years. They did not look very welcoming, either.

The peasants of the Westwood held their land from no lord and paid taxes directly to the crown. They were a rough, independent, stubborn people, who mistrusted outsiders and resented nobles who might try to claim their land and reduce them to mere tenants, owing rent and service for the land they themselves had cleared. I could sympathize with them, having longed so much for freedom myself, but right then I wished there were some knight's manor where we could seek protection.

Katerina began to reply. "Huvehla's grace be upon you…"

I elbowed her. She had taken charge, choosing when to stop and where, choosing which branch of every path to take. For all I knew, we could have been walking in circles. I had been feeling like a child again, afraid to whine lest she laugh at me, afraid to ask questions for fear of sounding ignorant. I had not even argued when she made a big fire every night, though I was more afraid of being found by my mother's knights than by warlocks—and anyway, a fire did not really keep away Nightwalkers, Lovell had said. But being mistaken for a Penitent missionary was too much.

"No," I said. "We're no missionaries. I'm a minstrel, the… the Rose Maiden, and this lady is my apprentice."

Minstrels were supposed to be grand and eloquent, butter and honey in their words. My voice shook.

"Minstrels?"

They did not believe me. Who would? I was a drab brown mouse.

No. My dress did not matter. I flung up my head.

"I'll play for you when your day's work is over," I said, and if my voice shook then, it was with anger as much as fear. "If you think I'm no good, you needn't offer us supper."

The man who had first spoken to me rubbed his muddy hands on his smock and stretched, an eye on the sun.

"Well now," he said, "the Rose Maiden, is it? Seems I've heard a song or two of yours when I was down to the mill in Narraford. I rather thought you'd be a bit…older."

I gave him a haughty look. He chuckled.

"Get along to the village and tell Aunt Nan in the old log house that Gregor said you'd like a bite to eat. You look dead on your feet. And this evening we'll see what good you are, girl."

I curtseyed in thanks and frowned at Katerina until she did likewise.

"Girl!" she muttered as we walked away, watched, I was sure, by every person in the field. Other people about their own work turned to stare as well, from other fields. "How dare he! Why did you let him?"

"He didn't mean to be unpleasant," I said. "What does it matter?"

"And what kind of food are we going to get in a place like this?" Katerina asked. "Look, Eleanor, there's no manor house, no lord over them. They live like…like outlaws."

"Hardly that!" I laughed, for the first time in what seemed like weeks. "They're free homesteaders. And I don't suppose we'll get any worse than what they eat themselves, so long as you keep from acting so superior and pious. They don't like Penitents, can't you tell? If you can put aside your piety to sing and dance when I play for you in the Old Keep, you can do it here."

"They're peasants," she protested.

"So might you have been, if Huvehla had woven differently," I said. "People are people."

"Don't quote your brother's heretic beliefs at me," she snapped. "If you're not any better than them, what are you?"

"A girl—a *woman*—who can make music," I said. "I hope."

The log house was shadowed with apple trees, overgrown with jewel-green moss, and seemed to be settling back into the earth from which its logs had grown. It was surrounded by beds of jumbled herbs, protected by fences of woven wattle from the flock of gray geese that grazed in the yard. Strong spicy spells filled the warm air. The geese announced us with loud hisses and shrieks, blocking the muddy path like so many fat-bodied snakes. The Rose Maiden could not be afraid of geese. I flapped my skirt at them and they gave way, one or two even retreating up a plank to the little woven goose-house on legs that stood by the door.

A mighty warrior. I grinned to myself and enjoyed the fact that Katerina, despite her swaggering and her dagger, was keeping safely behind me.

The noise of the geese brought Aunt Nan limping around the corner of the cabin, a basket of some gray-green leaves on her hip. She was an old woman, wizened as the apples we had taken, widow, we would learn, of the first man to settle here. In the one room of her house she clucked over our feet, insisted on smearing them with goose grease and fed us each two bowlfuls of a pottage of boiled lentils and greens, which Katerina polished off in no time flat. She also insisted on telling us the family history of every person in the tiny settlement, but that was a small price to pay.

When evening came and fear of the shadows chased people indoors, we ate a good rabbit stew and fresh bread with Gregor's family, even though they had not yet heard me play. And then the entire settlement, which was only a dozen families, gathered in their big threshing barn, with fires lit a safe distance outside the open doors in the two long sides to keep the warlocks away— though none of them seemed to fear the dark so intensely as Katerina did—and waited for me to make a fool of myself.

To tell the truth, I was the only one expecting that. I had lost all my courage. My hands shook. I wished I had not eaten so much at supper.

"I can't," I whispered, sitting crouched with my back against a post. "I can't do this. Katerina..."

A couple of the village women were lugging in crocks of ale. They gave me a curious look. A little boy stared with a finger in his mouth.

"Yes, you can." Katerina sat down beside me, an arm over my shoulders. "You can't anger them by backing out now.

Eleanor, dear, it's no different from playing for me. And they won't care—look at them. They want to have fun. They don't see many strangers. Even if you were terrible, they'd dance as long as they could find some sort of tune in it. And you're good. You know you are."

I shook my head.

"Oh, Eleanor." She looked around the barn. A couple of lanterns, burning no-doubt-precious tallow candles, hung from beams and cast pools of golden light on the stone-flagged threshing floor, and the bonfires beyond the doors flung in red streaks of light. People were staring, waiting, whispering. One man had a fiddle, a woman a tambour, a little hand drum. They looked ready to begin without me. Everyone was scrubbed and in their bright best. The girls all had ribbons in their hair. "Shut your eyes, if you have to. Play for your brother."

I swallowed hard, nodded and took out one of the flutes I had stuck in my belt.

When I stood, I had to lean against the post to hold myself up. I did shut my eyes.

I did not bother with the chatter of a real minstrel, the boasting and the lead-up to the song. I simply played.

It seemed forever before the fiddle joined in, and then the drum, and finally Katerina's high sweet voice. It was an old song, "For my delight is a summer's night, and a summer's day in the morning..." It was not, entirely, a song for polite company. I do not know why it came into my head. Perhaps it was the way a couple of the young people had been looking at one another.

After a while I opened my eyes.

It was like...I cannot find words to describe it. I felt as though I were taking on new life from the people in that barn, as if I were a tree, unfurling my leaves in spring, and they were the force of the spring in the earth and the sun, the spirit of the Fuallin-Queen who dances spring in with Jock Wildwood on

Fuallin-day, driving the last of winter out. It was as though I had never been alive before. The fiddler and I found one another's eyes and in our music danced together, trading the lead, playing chase. Katerina's voice wove through it and if she stretched a bit thin at times and hit a false note or two, nobody cared, and the fiddler and I came down to meet her and carry her along, while the drum called time for the dancers' feet.

They brought me mugs of ale to wet my throat, and Katerina danced with a curly-haired young man. Another youth asked me to dance, but I waved my flute at him and said no, I had to earn my hire, did I not, with a smile and a nod. He winked and blew me a kiss. A village girl gave me a look that was not quite friendly and grabbed his arm, so I played a slow sweet air for the two of them, and they danced together.

That night was magic. I carry it in my heart still.

One last five-step, my notes turning to breath a little, the fiddler's fingers fumbling. We were tiring. One last piece by the Rose Maiden, the starling's song, played without words. The fiddle and the drum stood arms about one another, silent, listening.

And then, in little family clusters, or holding hands, people wandered past the dying fires and home to bed.

"We can't pay you, Rose-girl," Gregor said, putting an arm around me and another around Katerina. "We can't afford to hire the Rose Maiden, not being lords with pockets lined with silver. But you've had your supper, and you'll have Aunt Nan's spare bed and your breakfast and food for the road, if you're going on, or you can stay if you like, as long as you want."

He swept us up to his wife, whose name was Young Nan, and she took my hands and kissed my cheek and said, "Rose dear, whatever you're running from, they won't find out where you've gone from us."

Was it so obvious? I was nearly asleep on my feet, or I might have protested. As it was, I let Young Nan take us off to Aunt Nan's, where Katerina and I fell into the bed in the corner of Aunt Nan's one-room cabin where Aunt Nan's children had once slept, all six of them. The mattress was a straw tick, not feathers, and the blankets were scratchy, but it all smelled of fresh lavender. Aunt Nan's snores were not enough to keep either of us awake, and even Katerina forgot to say her prayers.

❊ CHAPTER SEVEN ❊
ELEANOR: STRANGERS IN THE FOREST

I was woken by a shrieking like a damned shade. Panicked and not sure where to run, not even sure where I was, I stumbled out of bed in my shift. Then I recognized the sound as the geese, which had been shut into the little house on stilts for the night.

"Fox!" yelped Aunt Nan, bouncing like a girl from her own bed. "Vepris take it, a fox in my geese!"

"Whuzzzeh?" Katerina mumbled, and rolled over, making a cocoon of the blankets around herself.

A moment later she sat up, her dagger in her hand, as a man's voice called, "Powers bless the house," and someone pushed the door open.

The geese were silent again. Perhaps the shadow passing by their woven walls had woken them. Clear dawn light reduced the man to a dark bulk. Aunt Nan blinked.

"Who in Geneh's name are you?" she demanded, and picked up a stick of firewood. "Out! Out of my house right now!"

I stood frozen. The man took another step forward—a soldier in the black and yellow livery of the Baron of Sawfield. Another man loomed behind him.

"Your Highness? Lady Katerina?" The soldier bowed to me, then to Katerina. "I'm so glad to have found you. Your Highness, my lord baron has sent us to take you back to your father in Rensey."

"Highness?" Aunt Nan's voice rose into a squeak.

"No," I said. "You're mistaken. I'm not…"

"Maybe it's for the best, Your Highness," Katerina mumbled. "It's a long, long way to...to where you're going, and we're not doing well so far. We've already just about run out of food."

"I thought we were doing just fine," I said, my voice gone all thin and tight. "Or did you not notice I started to earn our way last night? I never expected it to be easy."

"Put some clothes on," Katerina said, in the same low voice.

I merely folded my arms, trying to look regal and defiant, which is not easy when one is wearing only a sleeveless shift of thin linen, very sweat-stained and wrinkled. When I glanced over, Katerina was sitting, head bowed, the blankets pulled up to her neck and the dagger out of sight again. I ought to have been as ashamed of my state of undress as Katerina, but I was angry instead. I was not the one who had forced my way into a stranger's house uninvited; I had nothing to be ashamed of.

"Sir," said Katerina, still keeping her eyes averted, "withdraw and allow us to dress. Your lord has given his word Her Highness will not be harmed, that she'll be treated with all honor and escorted back to her father in Rensey, yes?"

The man-at-arms gave a little bow and a smirk. "He has, my lady."

"Then she will accept the baron's safe-conduct to Rensey with thanks."

"No!" I said. "I will not!" But Katerina was right, I thought, as soon as the words were out of my mouth. We needed to seem meek and willing, so that we could escape at the first chance. We could not hope to resist two armed men. The villagers would not dare help us, even if they wanted to.

"We don't have time for this," the second man said, shouldering past the first and shutting the door behind him. "The queen's men are hunting her all over the west. Once we're out of the forest it'll be hard enough to avoid them as it is, without wasting half the day here on pretty words." He grabbed me by the arm. "We're taking you to the baron, as arranged, and he'll give you all the pretty words you deserve."

I screamed, loud enough to set the geese shrieking again, loud enough to start the dogs barking and bring the villagers, slow and foggy with ale and a late night, stumbling from their houses. I heard raised voices shouting to know what the matter was and the pounding of hooves. More soldiers? I twisted away, kicking and yelling even louder. I had nothing left to lose, not dignity, not the illusion of there being a peaceful and honorable escort.

"Eleanor, don't!" Katerina cried. "Don't! They mean you only honor. What choice do you have? We'd never make it through the Westwood, you know that. You don't belong up there with the kale-eaters and the Nightwalkers!"

Aunt Nan, with incredible bravery, hefted her stick of firewood again.

"You let that girl go!" she snapped. "No man's dragging a girl out of my house, princess or no!"

That was when someone heaved the door wide and hurled the man struggling with me across the room. The other whirled, drawing his sword, but a fist holding the hilt of a dagger struck his chin before the blade was clear, and he crumpled to the floor. The first soldier pushed himself to hands and knees, blinking, and looked up.

"Oh," said Aunt Nan, and sat down on her bed.

And *that* was when Katerina decided to scream.

"Shut up!" I snapped, and she was silent. We all were. Even the newcomer in the doorway did not seem to know what to say. He gave a sort of a shrug, looking around.

I have to confess I was staring. He was no giant, merely a tall, broad-shouldered, young man, but Aunt Nan's tiny cabin made him seem like one. He had needed to duck under the lintel. He looked like he might be someone's huntsman, dressed in leather leggings and a jacket that was probably, to judge by its rivets, a brigandine, lined with armor plates. He was no Eswyn native: a folded cloth of plaid in russet, white and blues was tucked into his belt in front and flung back over his shoulder. His hair was coppery red, worn in two long plaits, his beard unshaven. A Dunmorran Fenlander, I thought, and stared as if I were looking at some exotic beast in a menagerie. The left side of his face was marked by four long, ridged, white scars, where some huge-pawed animal had clawed him. A mercenary hired to kill me—except no, everyone wanted me alive, I forgot. He had not even bothered to draw his sword, just a dagger, as though a mere two soldiers were not worth the bother.

He gave my staring a lop-sided grin—the scars stiffened his lip and would not let him smile properly—and bowed. He might have winked, but his left eyelid was pulled crooked too. It was hard to tell.

He should have been ugly. He was not.

"Korby Moss'avver, at your service, madam," he said. He bowed to Aunt Nan as well, as though she were the lady of the manor.

She actually giggled. "Nan Holterswidow," she said and began arranging a shawl over her nightgown.

"Eleanor," Katerina said, in a dreadful voice, "you are wearing a shift."

Yes, and under the Fenlander's green eyes I felt as though the linen had turned to gossamer. I snatched up a shawl and felt my entire body flushing fiery red as I flung the garment around my shoulders and clutched it close.

Two more men crowded in the door, and the Fenlander made way for them. One was the villager Gregor; the other was a foreigner, the darkest man I had ever seen. His skin was deep brown. He wore a headdress of red cloth, though like the

Fenlander he wore practical leather leggings and a brigandine. He bowed gravely to me.

Did everyone know who I was? No one was bowing to Katerina.

"There are no others around," the foreigner told Korby in accented Ronish. He certainly was not a Ronishman.

Gregor had rushed to Aunt Nan. Their low hurried voices rose on words like "princess" and "the baron."

"No," said Korby, as the man who had flown across the room struggled up. "Stay." He took two strides and pushed him down again with his foot.

"You don't wish to return to Rensey with these men, Your Highness?" the foreigner asked me.

I shook my head, clutching the shawl close. I felt no more comfortable having him looking at me in my shift than I did the Fenlander. They were both quite young, and if the foreigner was not as tall as the Fenlander, he was still tall enough and had good shoulders and a handsome strong-boned face that I rather liked, once I stopped noticing how eerily black his eyes were. Even Katerina's brown eyes were remarked on, in Eswy. But his, thick-lashed under straight black brows, suited him very well...

I was an extremely wicked girl, obviously, to notice their looks so. A virtuous lady would have kept her eyes downcast and remembered she was betrothed.

"Since she doesn't want your company, out," the Fenlander said, with a jerk of his head towards the door. "Both of you in the wasp's livery, out. Let the ladies dress."

He and the foreigner, and after a moment Gregor, with a number of awkward bows to me, followed the stumbling soldiers out. I approved of the easy way the strangers each plucked a sword from Sawfield's men, without needing to discuss it and without any struggle or even protest. They were murmuring, heads close together, when Aunt Nan shut the door on them.

"Back door!" said Katerina, scrambling from the bed at last. "We can escape out the back."

"I don't have a back door, dear—madam, I should say," Aunt Nan said. "I suppose I shouldn't ask—"

"No, you shouldn't," Katerina said.

"Don't be rude," I told her, shaking out my gown. "What did the man mean, taking me to the baron *as arranged?*"

"How should I know? What are you accusing me of?" Katerina snapped, struggling into her stockings.

"What? I'm not! But—you were supposed to be skilled at this sort of secret travel, isn't that what you said? I thought you said you were making sure we didn't leave a trail? What use are you?" I was appalled to hear the words of the queen and her ladies coming from my own lips.

"I said I'd been taught; I didn't say I'd ever done it before!" Katerina yelled, and burst into tears. "It's all my fault. I'm sorry, Your Highness, I'm so sorry."

I flung my arms around her. "I'm sorry, Katerina, I'm sorry too. Don't cry. I didn't mean it. It's not your fault."

"It is, it is." Katerina wept, her face buried in her hands, her shoulders shaking. "I thought I'd hidden our trail so well."

She wiped her eyes on her gown. "But perhaps it's for the best. Perhaps it's Huvehla's will. The Baron of Sawfield will be a strong ally for your father, a strong protector for you. Better than being locked up in your uncle's court married to a child—you have no idea how dreary the court is in Hallaland—or ending up a victim of Nightwalker enchantment in Dunmorra."

"No," I said, and I began rolling up my bundle again, ready to go. "Don't speak of that again, Katerina, as you are my friend. I'm going to my betrothed husband in Dunmorra."

I kissed Aunt Nan's cheek.

"Thank you," I said. "We'll be on our way, while the foreign gentlemen are here to, um, distract Baron Sawfield's men. Could we buy some food, do you think? Things that will keep well." Katerina had money, I was certain. Katerina always had money. She would not have come on such a journey without a good purse of coin.

Really, now that I thought about it, it took only common sense, not any secret teachings from one's uncles, to know that a few pies were not the right sort of food to take on a long journey. It was a shock to realize that, much as I looked up to Katerina as beautiful, clever and worldly-wise, she was lacking in plain common sense. Either that, or she had believed I would give up after a couple of days. Did she really think me so weak?

I looked at her, tying up her own bundle. I could not believe she would be so devious as to trick me into turning back by arranging for us to run out of food. She would deceive my mother quite happily, but she was my friend. She had kept my secrets; she had come with me, when duty and her fear of the forest and Dunmorra said she should have betrayed me to my mother. If I could not trust her, whom could I trust?

But I could not depend on her, the secret part of my mind said.

"It'd be our honor to help you, Your Highness," Aunt Nan said. "If…" Her mouth set in a grim line. "No, even if this baron you're running from comes here himself, we won't say we've seen you."

I had sudden horrible memories of the story Lovell had told me about Baron Sawfield hanging a peasant without trial. "Don't defy him!" I said. "He's dangerous, he's cruel. Tell him we've gone into the forest, tell him we're heading for Dunmorra, tell him everything! He'll guess it anyway, and I won't have any of you hurt for my sake!"

"I'll talk to Gregor about food, Your Highness," Aunt Nan said, following us out into the herb-scented yard.

She paused to drag open the little door of the goose-house.

Gabbling happily, the fowl marched down the gangplank in a gray line.

"They'll follow us," Katerina said.

"The geese?" I asked.

"Sawfield's men." She nodded towards the rutted lane beyond Aunt Nan's wattle fences, where a crowd of villagers surrounded, at a wary distance, the four strangers and their horses. "They'll just pick us up as soon as we're out of the village, as soon as those two barbarian brutes let them go. It will be a lot better for us if we join them willingly."

Katerina might have been right, but I could not simply surrender. We could not sneak away without being seen, either. Everyone, every single pair of eyes, even those of the horses, seemed to be staring.

I raised my chin, hitched my bundle a bit higher on my shoulder and marched up the path to the lane. Katerina followed me, and Aunt Nan her. I suppose we looked a bit like the geese. The redhead grinned again.

"Thank you for you assistance, sirs," I said, with a polite, royally brief curtsey for him and his companion. "Powers bless you." And I turned to go around them, hoping Aunt Nan could shepherd some of her relatives after us, so we could get our food and get out of here. I had no real hope that we could escape, but pride would not let me tamely hand myself over to those soldiers. Especially now that they had their own injured pride, and probably injured bodies, to avenge.

Just when I thought we were actually going to be able to sidle by, Korby, who was holding the reins of several of the horses, gave one of them a thump with his elbow. The horse, a gray stallion with shaggy black feathering over its lower legs, a giant of the heavy Dunmorran Kordaler breed, backed up against the fence of someone's kitchen garden, blocking the lane.

"You should be glad you weren't worse hurt," the Fenlander said cheerfully to one of the soldiers. "Where I come from, we don't like it when men go dragging pretty girls from their beds in their nighties. Unless the pretty girl's cheerin' him on, a' course. And as for my lord, there, well, where he's from…" He shook his head. "You don't want to know what he thinks ought to be done about that kind a' thing. Throwing in the duckpond—and I see they got a good one—isn' the start a' it."

"You've made your last mistake, you and your jabbering fool of a lord," one of Sawfield's men said. "The baron's not a man you can expect to insult and get away with it."

"What's he saying?" the other soldier asked, staring at the foreigner. The dark man was murmuring in some language I did not recognize, a hand on the head of each of the two smaller horses.

"Ah, that's a Dravidaran blessing," the Fenlander said. "Very devout people, the Dravidarans. He's wishing you a safe journey back wherever you're going, praying for th' horses' feet to be sound and not go throwing shoes and stuff. I should have let him pray over mine, I guess, 'cause we've spent the last couple of days wandering around trying to find a smith, only came across one last evening, thank Ayas the man knew his trade, and the ladies ought to be thankin' sweet Mayn that we got an early start this morning and were riding by when we heard the racket—"

"Shut up, you clown," said Sawfield's man. "If you don't return our weapons to us, you'll find—"

"Can't do that." The Fenlander was so obviously enjoying himself that I would have laughed had I not been so scared. "Not the way you've been behaving. Now, my lord here, he was seriously thinking of cutting off your heads, which'd be a pity from your point of view, you have to admit, and buryin' you in the forest. So you see you're getting off lightly, just losing your swords and getting sent home, and a good devout Dravidaran prayer to speed you on your way. You know in Dravidara, there's a cult of priests make their living just prayin' for travelers? But he's a generous man, I es'pect he'll do this out of the goodness of his heart, in the hopes you'll find your own hearts opened to repentance and kindness—"

"Hey, no, keep your Phaydos-damned foreign jibberish to yourself," yelped a soldier, as the Dravidaran—Where under the sun was Dravidara? East of everything, I thought—turned and clapped a firm hand on each man's head. Just like my mother praying over me when I'd been particularly wicked as a small child, except the men were neither kneeling nor weeping. One stood as if frozen and the other tried to jerk away, but found the Fenlander's hand between his shoulderblades, holding him in place.

The Dravidaran finished his chanting and stepped back, bowing solemnly.

"There you are, all blessed," said the irrepressible Korby. "Off you go, now."

The two men-at-arms looked...strange. Wide-eyed and swaying a bit, clumsy as they mounted their horses. They suddenly seemed drunk. Everyone backed away as they turned their mounts' heads and trotted out of the village. No one spoke until they were safely past Gregor's turnip field, about to disappear under the eaves of the forest. Then, as one, everyone turned to look at the Dravidaran man.

"Strong prayers," said Gregor.

"That's Dravidara for you. I won't say my lord isn't known for a great philosopher in his own land." Korby winked and nodded. "The secret arts of the philosophers, eh? Come in handy now and then."

Gregor pursed his lips. "I see. Always thought the philosophers' secret arts had more, you know, writing things and drawing circles and such in 'em. So what did your lord the philosopher do to them, and how long before they come back with a few friends?"

The foreigners put their heads together, whispering.

"He says that he's sorry, but in an hour or two they'll remember they saw the princess somewhere—he couldn't do more than distract them for a little, not without doing their minds terrible injury—but they won't be able to lead any force of Sawfield's back to this village, and the memory will be confused, like a dream. So he hopes you'll be safe from those two, but if other men of Sawfield's chance across you, tell them what you have to about Her Highness's visit. Just don't go saying that those two had already been here, since they won't be able to say so themselves."

It was hard to tell if Gregor looked more relieved by knowing the soldiers would not be returning in a hurry, or worried by how it had been done.

The Dravidaran philosopher, or priest or whatever he was, turned to me.

"Your Highness," he said in good Eswyn, and then continued in careful Ronish. "I believe you said you were travelling to Dunmorra, Your Highness?"

Katerina, in the same language, answered before I could. "What you believe is your own affair, sirrah. Have the goodness to move your horses and your barbarian out of the way."

"I'm grateful for your help, sir," I said, ignoring Katerina. Why did she think she had to answer for me? "But my plans are my own concern."

"It so happens that we're travelling north ourselves," the man went on. "I am a scholar, studying the strange and, pardon me, barbaric customs of this land, particularly the tribe they call the Fenlanders."

His servant coughed.

"You clearly have enemies and need protection. I give you my word, with the Seven Powers to witness, that we are honorable men and will do everything in our power to bring you safely to your destination in Dunmorra."

The Fenlander gave a nod, his hand on the hilt of his sword, his lively face sober, as if by that gesture alone he too swore and took the oath seriously.

"Her Highness does not need—"

"Lady Katerina!"

"Your Highness," Katerina said meekly. "But—"

"Would you rather we were overtaken by Sawfield's men? Or the queen's?"

I did not point out that we had no way of resisting the armed strangers. I doubted that even the entire village would be able to oppose them.

"I accept your offer," I said. It was not I speaking; it was the Rose Maiden, daring, taking the reckless chance. If this was still a game of chess, what pieces were these two? And were they white or red? I did not think I was playing chess anymore, but some game for which nobody had told me the rules. There were too many sides, and I began to feel as though I were one all by myself.

"But I will not have you muttering your Dravidaran blessings over myself or my lady-in-waiting. I want that clearly understood."

"I do not think you are in need of my blessings," the Dravidaran said, and Korby snorted, which might have been boorish peasant manners, or might have been a suppressed laugh. With a glance at the villagers, I repeated my acceptance of the offer in Eswyn, so that they could understand. Most looked both worried and relieved: worried that I was throwing myself into worse danger, relieved I and my troubles were going away. I felt a bit the same myself.

"Eleanor, you can't be serious!"

I took Katerina's arm and pulled her aside. "What choice

do we have? They're not my mother's servants and they're not Sawfield's, and right now that's good enough for me. If they meant us harm, all they'd have to do is wait until we've left the village."

"There are a lot of strange stories about Fenlanders," Katerina said. "They live in a swamp and build houses out of mud. And they keep sheep in their houses and eat frogs and marry their own cousins."

"Well, I should fit right in with the last, then, shouldn't I?"

"And that wasn't any philosophers' art, that prayer."

"Have you studied the philosophers' secret arts?"

"No, but—"

"Then how do you know? I'm going with them, if they'll take me to Dunmorra. You can come, or you can turn around. Gregor and Aunt Nan will probably make sure you have enough food to get back to Narmor Castle."

"How can you be so hard, Eleanor?"

"I'm not being hard," I said. "I'm the crown princess of Eswy, and I will not let my kingdom be taken by Sawfield or by Hallaland. I'm using the weapons Anaskto the Protector of Kings puts into my hand, and right now, that is…these two…"

There I was, being the Rose Maiden again. And stumbling. I could not keep it up. I was terrified, excited, yes, all in one. And I had no idea of the allegiance of these men, no idea whom they served—was the foreigner a lord himself, or did he serve some Dravidaran prince who might take a side in Eswy's internal feuds? A battered shield was slung from the gray's harness, painted in stripes of blue and brown and white, the colors of the plaid, but it meant nothing to me if it meant anything at all, and the shield strapped among the baggage on the black's gear was the same, though the paint looked fresh.

Did scholars usually travel prepared for battle? Why was he carrying a shield in his servant's colors? That made no sense.

Something about these two was not right. But I could not see that I had any choice. I took a breath, unable to find the right ending to my grand speech, such as it was.

All the villagers were listening, as if I were a character in a play, a minstrel declaiming a tale. It was hard to tell what the foreigners thought. Probably they were trying not to laugh. The Dravidaran rescued me.

"Call me Marius," he said. "It's a Ronish name, but Dravidaran is a very difficult tongue. My man here is Korby. Shall we go?"

"The princess has not had breakfast," Katerina said stiffly.

"We should get as far from here as we can, as fast as we can, for the sake of these good people who've sheltered you," Korby said. His speech was all of a sudden much easier to understand than when he had been talking to the soldiers. He sounded a great deal more intelligent too, but perhaps that was my own prejudice.

"Is this what you want, Rose-girl?" Gregor asked. His sun-browned face turned brick-red. "Your Highness. I beg your pardon. Your Highness, do you really want to go with these men? Do you trust them?"

For the first time I noticed the heavy mallet he carried. Most of the men were armed with tools that were as good as weapons: hammers and axes and knives. Some of the women were too. My heart warmed. I was not alone. Eswy, the earth and blood and bone of Eswy, wanted me.

Well, the Rose Maiden could say so, at least in a song. In poetry even a lost cause and a battlefield feeding crows have a grim sad beauty. The Rose Maiden needed to remember that every one of those battlefield feasts for the crows had a name, a face, needed to think of Gregor and his kin, alive and dancing.

"I need to reach the king of Dunmorra," I said. "Eswy is in danger. You wouldn't have heard..." No, they would not have heard of Lovell's death, not yet, not in such an isolated place. I could not speak of it to them. I would end up weeping. "There isn't time to explain. But I need to go north to King Dugald, and Anaskto helping me, I will. I think, yes, that I do trust these men. At least they're not my enemies."

Gregor nodded.

"Those swords," Korby said. "I tossed 'em in the good grandmother's rhubarb patch. Take 'em and hide 'em well, all right? If you're going to have the smith back on the main track break them up for the steel, wait till the forest is quiet again. You don't want anyone to get caught with bits of those in scrap."

"Powers be with you and thank you, again, for your help," I said. "I'll always remember you. I'll always remember the dance."

After a bit of rearranging of harness and blankets to strap our bundles on and arrange pillions behind the saddles, the man who called himself Marius mounted the white-footed black stallion with the white face, and Korby tossed me up behind him. I grabbed the Dravidaran around the waist. I did not mean to. I could have gripped the cantle of the saddle. But the Kordaler stallion was just so tall, and if I fell, those massive hooves would crush me like an egg under a blacksmith's hammer. Katerina, perched stiffly behind the Fenlander on the gray, made a face as though she had just sipped vinegar.

Marius smiled at me over his shoulder, and my heart gave a peculiar lurch. I had never seen eyes so dark, so beautifully full of secrets—I really was a very wicked girl, and I did not let go of him, as the big Kordaler strode out, leading the way along a footpath that forded a muddy stream and angled across a hillside pasture. Sheep startled out of our way and a pair of grazing oxen watched with mild interest, and then the forest folded around us. It was like a ballad, I thought: the maidens saved from villainy by mysterious but honorable knights, carried off into the vast and trackless wild, where anything could happen—monsters, magicians, battles and true love…

"Rain coming this afternoon," Korby called behind us. "A good storm to wash our tracks away."

It never rains in the romances, when knights and ladies go on quests into the wilderness. Never.

✠ Chapter Eight ✠
Korby: Pursuit

"What were the two of you thinking?" I demanded of the lady-in-waiting, as we rode under the green twilight of the trees again. "Anyone would have thought you *wanted* to be followed. Dainty ladies' boot-prints that no one would ever mistake for a hunter's or a woodsman's in every puddle and damp bit of path, all those trampled ferns and broken twigs at every fork in the trail, and you didn't even bury the ashes of your fires!"

I glanced over my shoulder. The plump young woman sat as stiffly as a statue. She had a round pretty face, but she was going to grow into a saggy sullen old woman if she kept making that expression. The princess, in contrast, had been looking around her since we left the village, keen as a hunting deerhound and with a bit of the same lean sharp-boned elegance, her eyes alight with interest.

"You were spying on us," Lady Katerina accused.

"Ah, no, but we couldn't help noticing," I said hastily. "My lord's a scholar, after all. He notices things. We were curious. We thought, Well, here's a couple of young ladies alone in the forest—isn't that strange?"

The truth was, we had found it very strange, but Maurey had wanted to let the princess find her own way to Dunmorra if she could. "Let her spread her wings," was how he put it. "We'll follow closely, be there if she needs help, but if what her brother said of her life is true, maybe she needs to fly on her own for a bit."

"Needs, why?" I asked.

"Needs for herself. She's claimed her own life for the first time ever. I don't want to snatch that from her if I don't have to."

I'd have said no young woman should be wandering the Westwood like that, but when I thought what I was doing at her age, only a few years ago...I touched the troll scars on my face. If my cousin Oakhold hadn't set Maurey looking for me...But the Westwood wasn't the frozen mountains of Gehtaland, and there were no witch-trolls here. Would I trade what doubtful wisdom I'd won then to be a safe child again?

So maybe Maurey was right, but we made a mistake when Boots threw a shoe. We should have separated—one to find a farrier to reshoe the horse, the other to keep following the princess—but we didn't. The young women seemed in no immediate danger; we had seen no sign of pursuers other than ourselves, and we had not thought it would take long to find a smith on the main track heading towards the Narra valley, even leading a three-shoed horse. Unluckily, by the time we had caught up again, so had a couple of the baron's men. I suppose they decided they didn't want to drag the princess away from a crowd of happily tipsy woodsfolk, who might object to their celebration being interrupted, and that was why they waited around until morning. Their mistake made up for ours, and we had already broken camp at dawn, ready to move out whenever the princess set off. Or to ride to the rescue, which was the most fun I'd had in days.

Four days after, we were deep in the Dunmorran Westwood, still south of the main track to Greyrock Town, in a deserted region with nothing but deer and elk paths winding through it. The forest was all bog-larch, poplar and birch, with deep moss, bracken and wiry grass between them. Warblers sang, and the sunlight spilled golden around us. I was tired and cranky, though, and fed up with Lady Katerina.

The princess herself was a fair companion for travel. She was polite; she was interested in seeing new things. She had us show her how to start a fire and cook a supper stew of cracked wheat and dried meat; she glowed with quiet pride when I let her make the porridge one morning and it turned out to be edible. She helped gather firewood and tidy the camp. It did cross my mind that she was trying to learn what she needed to know for when she ran away from us. She also asked questions about the trees and the animals, about Dunmorra and Dravidara. Maurey grew inventive; when he ran out of facts—the only book he'd ever read about Dravidara had been very short—he made it up. Eleanor listened solemnly, taking it all in.

And shyly, in the evenings, the princess made music for us. She lent beauty even to her drab and shapeless gown as she played, her eyes half-closed, sculpted face transcendent, like a holy woman hearing the music of the Powers' heavenly dance. Dugald was a lucky man, I thought, if he could make her happy.

But Lady Katerina fussed over the princess like a nursemaid and used her title to bludgeon us with the girl's importance and our own unworthiness. "Don't sit there, the ground's damp. One of you put down a cloak for the princess." "Are you sure you should eat that, Your Highness? It's a very peculiar color,"—as I offered, on the end of my knife, a chunk of good sheep's-milk cheese, marbled with sage the way my sister makes it. "Don't lie down *there*, Your Highness." "Come away from that horse. It looks savage." As if any Kordaler had ever been anything but an overgrown puppy, away from battle! "You don't need to know that, Your Highness, it's *not* your job to make fires." "Your Highness! Let him scrub the porridge pot himself. It's his job." Eleanor endured it as if she hardly noticed.

It didn't take a witch to know Katerina resented us. Maybe she was afraid the princess would grow out of being dependent on her, and she would lose her importance. Maybe her love was the possessive kind that can't stand it when someone else, anyone else, matters. I couldn't swear to her reasons, but her jealousy was strong, like bile in the throat. Try riding with that seething behind you. And jealousy wasn't all that made the lady-in-waiting an uncomfortable companion. Lady Katerina feared the forest, with its strange noises and sudden movements; she also had some great guilt gnawing at her heart. I couldn't tell what she felt guilty about. It seemed something deeper than merely her clumsiness in allowing Sawfield's men to track them, something older. I would have been sorry for her, maybe tried to ask her why she hid such unhappiness, tried to show her the way to walk out of it and set it aside, if she didn't so obviously despise me as a near-barbarian peasant, not fit to share a fire with her lady.

Eleanor was riding with me that afternoon, though Katerina had protested, it not being fitting for the princess to ride with a mere servant, as she thought me.

"But Master Marius wouldn't know about the Fens, Katerina," Eleanor had said to that. "And I need to learn about all of Dunmorra, not just the people of Cragroyal that my brother met."

There have been kings of Dunmorra who couldn't be bothered to make that much effort, though they never failed to send the assessors to count our flocks (those they could find, hah!) and demand their taxes.

I explained about clan tartans and why Fenlander warriors didn't have their own personal devices for their shields like knights but just used the colors of their clan, the way Nightwalkers used the emblem of the House to which they owed allegiance. That led to her asking about Nightwalkers, which brought a surge of anxiety from Katerina. Interesting, I thought, my mind only half on what I was saying. Katerina listened intently while pretending not to. Indignation flared off her now and then, when something I said annoyed her particularly. Very interesting. It seemed to me that she'd have been snapping contradictions, except that she didn't want to let on she thought herself an expert.

Why should a Penitent girl, and a Hallalander at that, have opinions on Nightwalker society and customs? What did Hallaland have to do with Nightwalkers at all? It might be worthwhile sending someone to pry into Lady Katerina's family background, I was thinking, while I explained how every Nightwalker belonged to a House, and though they usually belonged to the same one their family always had, there was no reason people could not transfer their allegiance—if they married someone from another House, say, or had some other reason for a closer relationship.

Gradually, though, something else began to press on my thoughts. I became certain we were being followed.

There were no settlements or even single steadings in this part of the forest—the soil was too poor and boggy to be worth farming. The emotions that I began to feel, eddying away and back like the edge of a rising tide, were those of a large number of people, their attention keen and focused. I broke off my lecture.

"My lord Marius," I said, in my vile Ronish—Maurey was still being a Dravidaran traveler, though I had noticed the alchemical dye was beginning to wear off his hands. I switched to Gehtish, which I doubted either of the girls knew. We didn't know that much ourselves, but enough for what I needed to say. "Trouble. Men hunting behind. Many."

"Hunting?" he asked and then nodded understanding. A large party in the Westwood, and not on the main track from

Cragroyal to Greyrock Town, was unlikely to be anything but trouble looking for Eleanor.

"Oh, was that Dravidaran?" Eleanor asked with interest.

"Gehtish," Katerina corrected, and bit the word off as if she regretted it.

Damn.

It might have been possible for me to wish a bit of confusion on one or two pursuers, muddle them so they missed the too-obvious hoofprints, but to affect that many minds would take a dozen witches. Maurey snapped twigs from a whippy larch as we rode beneath and began weaving something, whispering a spell, while Katerina demanded, "What's that? What are you doing? That's not any sort of philosopher's art, that's…"

The prince flung the woven framework of the spell behind us with a word—something to misdirect anyone tracking us.

It didn't have a chance to do any good. Katerina's mind exploded with a cloud of terror and she shrieked, "Nightwalker! That's *warlock* magic! Eleanor, run! Run!" She flung herself from Boots' back as Maurey, too late, grabbed for her. The girl landed on hands and knees, bounced up screaming and slashing at Maurey with her dagger as he leaned down to snatch at her and then bolted towards me, shouting till the forest rang, "Eleanor! Eleanor, warlocks, get away!"

Harrier knew what to do about people running screaming at him waving steel. He wheeled, leaving me room to strike, but I was too busy grabbing Eleanor, who had slid as Harrier lurched. She grabbed me too and clung on, hanging down the side of the horse, but if I let go she'd fall. Stupid notion, that women have to ride in skirts. Harrier struck at Katerina himself, and I hauled him aside at the last moment, poor beast, while Katerina tumbled sprawling, trying to avoid Harrier's hooves. She lost her dagger, clawed her way out of the snarl of raspberry canes she had landed in and snatched at Eleanor's ankle as I tried to drag the princess up before me, a more secure seat with the horse dancing around, confused and angry.

"What in Huvehla's name—?" Eleanor demanded, as confused as Harrier. "Katerina! Let go! They're not our enemies. What on earth's the matter with you?"

Katerina shrieked once more, in anger this time, turned and fled, hoisting her skirts up to her knees. "Help!" she shouted. "Help! Help! Warlocks!"

"Let her go," Maurey said, though I hadn't made a move to follow. The princess and I were trying to sort out the tangle we'd gotten into, as I dragged her from behind to before. Clasped close against my chest, she looked up once, flushed, and grabbed Harrier's mane.

"I won't let you fall," I promised, and dismounted, settling her in the saddle. Her nerves jangled with shock and fear, but she didn't try to flee, and she didn't call after Katerina. I soothed Harrier's ruffled nerves and apologized for yanking on his mouth so hard, let him slobber affection and "apology accepted" over my braids, while I looked for Katerina's dagger. When I stooped to pick it up, something else caught my eye: a black ribbon dangling in the raspberries. I picked it up too. It had worn thin, easy to tear, but it still carried what I first would have ignored as some amulet of Huvehla the Weaver, until I remembered that Penitents disdained any sort of jewellery as vanity.

"What is it?" Maurey asked, seeing me frowning. He rode over, Boots treading delicately, ears swivelling, alert for more enemies.

Feeling Eleanor's eyes on me, I handed over the dagger, with the amulet bundled in my palm.

"Take a look at that," I said, "when we've got time."

I felt his surge of tension. "Interesting," was all he said, though. I blocked Eleanor's view as he took it and stowed it away out of sight.

Symbol of the Yehillon. The thin, tarnished silver disc that the canes had torn from Katerina's throat bore the same pattern as the medallion of the man I had killed in Hallasbourg Library.

"Have you ever heard the name Yehillon, Your Highness?" I asked, and such was Maurey's distraction that he answered with Eleanor, "No," and went on, "I told you…"

"Who's Yehillon?" Eleanor asked warily.

"I was hoping you knew."

"What Katerina said. Master Marius, are you…?"

Maurey shrugged.

"What were you doing?"

"Setting a spell to confuse your pursuers for a few hours. Katerina managed to trample it," he added ruefully.

"You're not from Dravidara."

Maurey shook his head.

"You have a Dunmorran accent, but your Eswyn's as good as mine. You don't look like a Nightwalker. Was she right, though?"

Stiff dignity in her posture, fear in her voice.

"King Dugald sent us to help you, Your Highness," I said. "Your father asked for his help for you."

"My father did?" Her face lightened, and so did her mind, as her fear eased. "You're his *brother*!" she said to Maurey. "King Dugald's brother, er, Lord Maurey, yes? Prince Maurey, I mean. But Lovell said you didn't look human."

"The brown's a particularly nasty-smelling alchemical…"

"Gunk?" I supplied.

"Gunk that a friend of mine invented. It washes off with special soap. Or so he says." Maurey unwound the turban and shook his hair loose. "That's better. Your Highness, there's a large company"—he glanced at me and I nodded—"a large company of men getting fairly close to us. Even if they didn't hear that shrieking…"

"Katerina will run into them. We have to save her!"

"Katerina's running *to* them," Maurey said gently. "It's plain she's known you were being followed all along. Your Highness, she's betrayed you. You need to decide, right now—"

"No! She wouldn't. Not Katerina. She's…she's my friend, my only friend. She's been a sister to me. She's…she's only scared. She's been brought up Penitent, you see."

"So have you," I pointed out, "but you def'nitely turned out better." Maurey gave me a quelling look.

"Well, whether she meant betrayal or not, it's clear she thinks you'd be better off in Baron Sawfield's possession or your mother's than with us. Will you still accept our escort to Dugald, or will you go back to Eswy with whoever's behind us? And you should know, before you decide, that we have information that your brother's death was no accident. I'm sorry," he added, with gentle awkwardness, "I couldn't tell you before, when I was being Marius. I didn't know your brother long, but during the time Lovell spent in Cragroyal, I enjoyed his friendship. He was a good companion. And he spoke very highly of you. He loved you dearly, but you know that."

For a moment I thought she would cry. She blinked hard and then stared at us, those winter-sky eyes wide and shadowed with the weight of the choice and all that hung from it. Her lips thinned.

"Thank you," she said. "I'm not stupid. By my brother's grace, I'm not even uneducated. Men do die from falls, but Lovell would not have been drunk, as they said he was, and his death was far too useful to too many people. I know my brother was murdered, but not by whom. And I would like to know your proofs."

"Later," Maurey promised.

Oh, that was going to be tricky to explain. Penitents were probably not that fond of witches, either, if they could be brought to believe in them at all.

"Your Highness, your enemies are nearly on us."

The sensing of people's hearts is like hearing: in an isolated place, empty of the clamor of other lives, sound and emotion carry farther. They weren't that close, but still, too close to linger here any longer.

Eleanor didn't ask how we knew. Probably she thought it was Nightwalker magic.

"I'm going to Dugald," she said. "Your Highness, um, Korby. If you please."

Maurey gave her a little bow from the neck, Nightwalker fashion, and I unstrapped my shield from Harrier's baggage, settling it into place on my arm, ready. "You can call me 'my lord' too, if you like," I said generously, as I mounted behind her. We didn't discuss who would take Eleanor. I could probably do better in a running fight, cumbered with a passenger to protect, than Maurey. "Just so we're all being formal together."

However weakly, she did laugh, as I intended. I could get to like making her laugh, I decided.

Maurey had his shield ready too, and loosened his sword in its scabbard. I wished I had my armor, and Harrier's. The brigandine, a jacket lined with horn plates rather than steel, Fen-style, was fine for the sort of tussle we had thought we might run into, but taking on a baron's troop of men-at-arms—in proper plate, Harrier and I would be worth a dozen light soldiers.

No point wishing for the moon, as my mother says. Be glad you've got a rush-light.

With Eleanor held close before me, in no danger of sliding off, I set Harrier to a pounding canter. Boots followed close, with Maurey watching the brilliant, sun-dappled afternoon forest, searching not for movement but for deep shadows. None dark enough. Evening twilight could not come too swiftly. The emotions of the men seeking us stirred, roiled like a muddy pool disturbed. Perhaps they'd met Katerina. I couldn't distinguish individual minds. The heat of their excitement was enough to warn me they thought they had us.

✠ Chapter Nine ✠

Korby: No Escape

They caught up only a few miles later, though Maurey had thrown another spell or two behind and I was wishing confusion on them with all my will. Neither sort of magic used this way has much strength against hard certainty, though. They knew we were ahead of them, and they had the massive hoofprints of the Kordalers in the moss to follow, as well as a very strong will of their own to find us, so turning them aside would have taken serious spell-working of a kind we had no time for. The shadows grew longer as the afternoon wore on, but none gave any true darkness yet. So much of the Westwood is mile upon mile of ancient oaks and elms, maples and pines, their dense branches creating an unending evening. Just our luck for our enemies to catch up in this stretch of open woodland, where it would have to be true night before Maurey could enter the halfworld.

"Two dozen," I called to Maurey, looking behind. "Light horse and light armor. Only a couple of archers." They were spread out in a loose skein, sweeping up from the side, hemming us in. Their mounts could outrun my Kordalers, and had.

"Those are Baron Sawfield's colors," Eleanor added, catching sight of a rider in black and yellow. She tried to lean around me. "Is Katerina?…She's with them. She's riding with Sawfield himself."

Harrier rose and lifted over a long smooth hummock, moss overgrowing pale stone, and a few strides farther on and to the side, Boots soared over another. A third leaned, like the branchless ruin of a wind-driven tree, tall as Harrier's head. We dodged it as an arrow hissed by and shattered against the stone. Behind us, Katerina screamed and a man roared anger. That's right. No shooting the princess, idiots.

More stones were scattered among the lacy larches. Many had fallen. They weren't pillars or monuments carved and finely shaped, but they weren't natural, either. I remembered seeing something similar once north of the Fens, a deserted place on a sea-cliff where ancient stones leaned and fell, forgotten. Rings of them. And the inner ring was most closely spaced, almost a wall, a place we could defend, maybe, if this was the same. A place to trap the darkest evening shadows, if we could hold it so long. But which way were these circling? The Yerku send that they hadn't all fallen. I spotted another upright stone and called to Maurey to head for where the ground began to rise. A man on a speedy little horse hurtled at me from the right, grim-faced, and we turned on him, but Maurey and Boots were there, charging between him and the princess. Eleanor cringed back against me at the scraping clash of steel on steel, and I wheeled Harrier away, taking the lead up what seemed to be a low sandy mound, where birches grew thick. So did the stones, some fallen, nearly buried, some still upright but crazily leaning. Sawfield's man fell and the horse bolted, but two more closed on Maurey. He spun Boots away and pounded after us, weaving through trunks and stones. They did shoot at him, but their arrows missed. Might have been a spell.

The ring of stones I had hoped to see was there—flattish slabs, lumpen boulders, tall narrow columns, mostly upright. Trees had heaved some aside, tilted others, and, as Harrier crashed through what I thought was probably a gateway into a ring filled with birch and jack pine, I realized it wasn't like the place I had seen after all, where the one original gap in the wall had faced to the southwest. This had four narrow gaps, north, south, east and west, and there were only two of us to hold them. Boots thundered in, and Maurey saw at once what we had to deal with—four places to defend and the ring too thick with young trees to fight very effectively on horseback if anyone did break through. He slid down and ran to the west, grabbing up a pair of dead branches as he did so. He wedged them across the western gap, stood, hands on them, chanting in Talverdine. The air wavered and grew thick, murky and gray. Stone. An illusion, but a good one. So long as nobody picked that point to climb it would hold. He did the same for the north and east, and by then Sawfield's men were trampling up the hillside in our wake.

"That'll keep them from trying those gaps while I come up with something better," Maurey said. "Hold the south till I call you back."

I saluted him with drawn sword and dropped Eleanor down on her feet.

"Stay by Maurey," I ordered, and rode out so that I was just before the gateway.

Sawfield's men formed up in a crescent, himself in the center. Katerina slid down.

"What have you done with Her Highness?" she demanded.

I wasn't there to argue, and I didn't think she deserved an answer. I waited, sword in hand, watching the men-at-arms, listening, if you can call it that, to their hearts, their anticipation, their dog-hungry urge to fight.

"Release the princess to us, and you can ride away from here, sirrah," Sawfield called, while Katerina shook her head in violent contradiction. Did she think better a dead princess than a live warlock?

"Korby, there's a fallen stone in the center here," Maurey called. "Carved! Old Talverdine syllable-symbols. Er, Ros…Vey. No, it reads the other way. Veyros. That's the Great Power of the

Sun, Phaydos." Believe it or not, for a moment, he was lost in the excitement of that discovery.

"Is that important, Your Highness?" I heard Eleanor asking doubtfully. "Will it help?"

"No, but I've never heard of anything like this in the Westwood. It's so far from the usual tracks and so boggy, I suppose people don't come this way very much, so it's never been reported—"

"If you want to play university master, wait till we've dealt with these fools!"

"Sorry, Korby," he called, sounding amused.

I went back to giving off an air of being mysterious, dangerous and possibly not even anything of this world. Witchery. A trick I learned from my sister, who used to reduce me to tears by it, when I was about four and she was old enough to know better, almost a woman grown—until my father caught her at it. Anyway, it made Sawfield's men reluctant to come any closer, and every minute we could hold them off would matter as the afternoon fell into the long golden Therminas evening.

Sawfield gathered his men around him, gave orders, and a handful of them scattered into the woods on either side, circling the hill. The others moved restlessly, watching me.

"Kale-eating warlock-lover!" one called, but his heart didn't seem in it. I was worrying them. Good.

When I failed to answer their taunts or be drawn away from the gap I guarded, they came. No lances. A slow uphill charge. Their plan was clear. While several engaged me, others would get through the gap and deal with Maurey. I didn't let Harrier plunge forward as he wanted, didn't leave them space to dodge around me.

Like us, they weren't in full armor, but a mix of brigandines and mail, lightweight compromise for long travel without a baggage-train. Only Sawfield and his captain wore breastplates, and they weren't the ones swarming me; they, Katerina and a handful of guards to protect them, stayed well back out of it.

Horses whinnied angry challenge and squealed, hooves and teeth almost as dangerous as swords. I caught slashing blows on shield, on sword. A man slumped, blood spurting from his neck. His horse, trapped and panicked between Harrier and more wasp-liveried attackers, reared and threw him under the milling hooves. Harrier reared and lashed at a soldier before me, struck him with a flailing hoof, and that meant two riderless horses packed close against me, in the way of the attackers and causing their own bit of mayhem, but there were enough other swords hacking at me to keep busy.

They would bring me down, and it wouldn't take long. Even though only a few could come at me at a time, there were too many to guard against, too many to fight off, and I had nowhere to run. I was dimly aware, through the storm of their excitement, of Maurey afoot behind me, chanting sing-song Talverdine.

"They're coming over the wall!" Eleanor screamed, and then a man yelped and she shouted. Her fear and anger lanced through the deafening—that's not the right word, but it's close enough—deafening emotions drowning me, but Maurey went on chanting. I couldn't spare a glance back. Harrier's shoulder was bleeding; so was I, I knew, arm and thigh, and my sword-arm was growing weak. For every man I wounded there was a fresh one to take his place.

"Now!" Maurey roared. "Moss'avver!" I spun Harrier, and we hurtled through the gap. It roared up in flame behind us. The entire ring of stones burned, not just the four gateways. One of Sawfield's men crouched inside the stones, retching. Eleanor stood a safe distance away, her back to Boots' black shoulder, hands before her mouth.

I slid down and leaned on Harrier, panting. My leg was bleeding in two places as well as my arm. The horses snorted and stamped as the fire climbed higher, and Boots backed up, ears flat. Eleanor caught his reins, but his eyes were rolling. He'd pull her right off her feet and hardly notice her weight.

"Shh, shh, boys," I said. "It's all right." Witchery behind the words soothed them, quieted their growing fear. Wind gusted around us, lifting the horses' manes, stirring the leaves, which were browning and curling. Bark charred and began to smoke. My hand was stuck to the hilt with drying blood.

"What's it burning?" I asked, kneeling down to wipe my sword on the grass. The fire was no illusion, and too hot to be any kind of magician's fire of the sort Maurey summoned to shed light.

Maurey nodded at the tree nearest him. As I watched, its small twigs crumbled to ash and sifted away on the wind. Branches began to crumble as they fed flames twenty feet distant.

"Very impressive."

"Say that once we've figured out what to do next. I may have just trapped us here." He looked over at Eleanor. "Well done, Your Highness, thank you."

"What did you do?" I asked her.

"The soldier. I hit him with a stick, and he fell off the wall," she said, sounding dazed. "And then he grabbed me. So I hit him again. Um, with my knee. Like Lovell told me." She flushed.

"Good for Lovell," I said.

"Give me a hand," Maurey ordered, and as Sawfield's man struggled to his feet again the two of us heaved him up and over the stones where the flame was lowest.

"All this fire isn't going to bring on the good deep shadows any faster, though," I pointed out.

"A slight flaw in my plan we can deal with later," the prince conceded. "You're hurt, Korby. Let me see."

"It'll keep." I pulled away from him, checked Harrier. He had one deep cut I didn't like the look of, though the bleeding had slowed, and a good few scratches and swelling bruises. My cousin swears by a goosegrass salve, but I find witchcraft is better for keeping a wound sweet and clean, and I did what I could for Harrier, my hands on his hot hide either side of the cut, forehead pressed to his sweating neck, letting the world go dim and distant while I sank myself in the healing. I know how fast a cut like that can fester and weaken even a strong and healthy beast, what with dirt and sweat and flies, and I didn't intend losing Harrier. Such witchcraft sucks the strength from you, though, almost as if what goes into the healing comes straight from your soul, and I was craving sleep the way a drunkard does wine, by the time I was done. I slid down to my knees, but the slash on the stallion's shoulder was scabbed over, old and black.

There are stories of witches who could heal real wounds, mortal wounds, cure fatal illness. Always long ago and in some other clan. No one I know has ever cured anything that wouldn't have healed on its own, with luck and time and good care. Witching's a shortcut when it comes to such things, that's all.

So I'm like an old granny with her cats when it comes to my horses. Maurey didn't point out that this had perhaps been a foolish and reckless waste of energy. "*You're* still bleeding," was all he said, ripping that red cloth from his turban into bandages to tie over the bloody sleeve and my leg, with a quick spell in Talverdine which could speed healing, though not nearly so swiftly as what I'd done for Harrier.

"What now?" Eleanor asked, her voice tight. I suppose, watching us, she was beginning to wonder if we'd forgotten where we were and what we were doing.

"Rest," I said, forcing open an eye to check the height of the sun. "Can't do anything for another hour at least." I lay back on the grass. Harrier, with a sigh, started to graze by my head, making a mess of his bit, but I was too weary to care.

"We can't just sit here."

"Yes, we can. They can't get in. We can't get out. We sit here."

"Until the fires go out," she said.

The smaller branches and the saplings were mostly consumed now and the bigger trees were burning, if you could call it burning, when they and the flames they were feeding were yards apart. The tallest jack pine was smouldering, its needles dissolving from green to ashen dust, its branches to charcoal, while the flames danced over the stones.

"We wait until the western stones there cast enough shadow for me to take us into the halfworld," Maurey corrected Eleanor, sitting down as well. "While you're up, grab the waterskin off Boots, will you? Thank you."

She didn't protest; it was a request any one of us might have made of any other, and I was pleased Eleanor saw it that way. She brought the skin of water and some oatcakes, and the other two made a meal of sorts, though I fell into a doze after only a swallow of water.

"He's a witch," I vaguely heard Maurey explaining. "You know there are witches in the Fens? It makes him tired."

I tried to wake up enough to thump him or at least glower and snarl that it wasn't nearly so simple as that, but my body didn't seem to find it worth the effort, and the next thing I knew the princess was shaking me.

"Maurey says to wake up," she told me, and I rolled to my feet. Despite the dancing whirl of light from our hedge of fire, the shadows cast by the sun were stretching long across the circle. Not dark enough though. I've never regretted the long days of midsummer so much.

The prince was at the southern gap, too close to the fire. He reeked of smoke when he walked back. The horses shied away from him.

"They're up to something out there," he said. "Digging."

"Earth," I said at once. "They'll put the fire out at one of the gaps."

"They won't need earth," said Eleanor. "Think of how boggy it is down there. Wet moss—it'll be like soggy wool, and they can scrape up bushels of it." We both looked at her. She flushed, hunched up, wrapping her arms close. "I'm sorry, I just thought…," she began.

"You're right," Maurey said. "I never thought of that. Faster than digging, wetter, lighter to carry…They're piling it on shields and cloaks."

Harrier seemed sound, though probably the scab was going to pull a bit. The Yerku grant it didn't reopen. I took my shield again, swung into the saddle.

"You take Eleanor on Boots, m'lord," I said. "Run for it. Don't wait for me."

"*Such* a Fenlander plan. A big fight, a retreat, and everybody dies in the end anyhow."

We both whirled around, swords hissing free. A man on a white horse stared down his nose at those of us still on the ground, ignoring me, as he'd have had to stare up. Sharp nose, ears you couldn't miss, sharp chin he tried to hide with a little beard…

"*Idiot!*" said Maurey. "*Powers*, you idiot! You could have dragged the princess into the halfworld and taken her away."

"What princess?" asked Romner, properly Lord Romner, a friend of my lord's, the Powers know why, and the second-most grating person I know after my Aunt Linna. He jumped down, soothing his mare with a hand on her nose. She didn't like the fire any better than Harrier and Boots did. I was impressed he'd got her to jump through it, even in the halfworld, where it would be a mere ghost of burning.

Romner studied Eleanor and didn't seem impressed, but he looks that way at everyone. My cousin says he doesn't mean it, but I'm not so sure. "Are you collecting human women now, Your Highness? Annot's not going to like that. At least this one doesn't have orange hair."

"Her Highness, the Crown Princess of Eswy," I said, making introductions. "Lord Romner of House Rukiar. Don't mind him, Your Highness. He's rude to everyone."

Eleanor curtseyed, very correctly, if nervously, trying to study the Nightwalker without being seen to stare. Romner bowed.

"Don't mind the Moss'avver," he told her. "He isn't housebroken yet. Maurey, Her Grace the queen wants you at this meeting at Greyrock, Veyros knows why, nobody tells me. Being expert at making Maurey-finding devices"—he dangled from one hand what looked to me like a crazy cat's-cradle of fine thread, which I suspected was partly the prince's hair—"of course it was me they sent to fetch you. Though I was expecting you to be off in Rensey."

"Things got interesting."

"So I see. How are you making the fire, by the way? Is it burning these trees in here? Fascinating."

"It's a variation on the theory that—" Maurey switched to Talverdine, and Eleanor and I looked at one another.

"When the warlocks have quite finished their little chat, they might rescue us," I told her. "But I wouldn't count on it. You have any brilliant ideas?"

"He came out of the halfworld. There wasn't anyone there, and then he was."

"Yes, they do that."

"But if he got out, why can't he go back?"

"Darkness," I said. "Darkness is the door in, though you can step out anywhere. And Maurey's right, if Romner'd stayed put, he could have pulled you in too and gotten you away without them seeing you."

"How was I to know?" Romner asked, aggrieved. "If you want people to rescue princesses for you, you need to let them know beforehand. From outside, I thought those humans were trying to burn you in here."

"We're both quite capable of putting an ordinary fire out," I said.

"So are Sawfield's men," the princess pointed out. "Listen."

It was hard to hear over the crackle of the flames and the roar of the wind that the fire sucked past us, but there were voices.

"All around us," I said, giving up on listening with my ears. "They're going to fling down wet peat like the princess said and come in all four gaps at once…" Maurey's stone-illusions were gone, burned in his own fire. "They're not going to let us wait till dark. They're very confident."

Maurey was watching the southern gap, his eyes grim.

"I can stop them," he said. "The rest of you get out of here, ride down anyone in your way and get as far as you can."

"No," Romner and I said together, knowing what he meant to do. That wild uncontrolled power unleashed could just as easily kill him as any men rushing the ring. And what it would cost him, to kill so savagely…

"Neither of you should be let out without a keeper," Romner said. "Eleanor, Your Highness, your foot."

"My—?"

He heaved her up the side of the white mare, grabbed her right leg and shoved it over even as she protested. She glowered, her face burning, her skirts dragged up around her thighs as Romner shortened the stirrups for her.

"Don't worry, I'm not in the least interested in human women or their legs," he assured her, which wasn't true, and Eleanor did have legs worth a look. He flung his own cloak around her and pinned it—bright red, hooded and a sharp contrast to her dull brown gown and shawl. "Now, hold on. Use your legs. Keep yourself centered. Don't rein her in. Don't worry, she's smarter than the human breeds of horse and some humans."

"You better not be looking at me, Lord Romner."

"And faster than anything on four legs I saw down there. Her breed can enter the halfworld on their own, and that's what she's going to do, run for it and take you in at the first good shadows she comes to. Go north until you come to the Greyrock track. You should recognize it: It has become nearly a proper road these days, broad and rutted. Go west. Don't come back looking for us. The king is on his way to meet my queen at Greyrock Castle. If he isn't there yet, they'll help you up at the castle. Understand?"

"Yes, but…"

"Good. Look after my horse. Her name is Sennanna. There's food in the saddlebags, grain for Sennanna."

Romner held the mare's head, murmuring to her face to face in Talverdine. No animal could remember that long an instruction. It was a spell, or a series of commands and impulses laid into her, which would govern her actions. I could almost see how it was done. Closer, maybe, to witchery than the usual warlock magic is.

"Here they come," I warned the others. "Smallest group's at the east."

"Damp down the fire at the east," Romner said, and we both did, I with witchcraft, willing the flames to sink and die, and Maurey with a two-handed gesture and a few words.

Romner slapped the white mare's flank and spoke again, and though the angle of her ears said she was unhappy, she gathered herself and leapt the sinking flames in the eastern gap, scattering a handful of men afoot who had not been expecting us to make a sally. It took them a moment to realize someone was fleeing, and by then it was too late. "Nightwalker!" they screeched, "Warlock!" And they did not cry, as they should have done, "The princess is escaping!" The lean light Talverdine horse and her rider were a flash of silver and scarlet dodging through the trees, heading north.

The flames roared up again. A pair of riders tried to follow the white horse, but they hadn't a hope of overtaking, so long as Eleanor did not fall. It was out of our hands now, anyway.

"A quarter of an hour," Maurey said. "That long, maybe, till the shadows of the western stones in here grow dark enough. If we didn't have so many gaps to defend...Romner, help me. We're going to move some stones."

I was busy. The first loads of sodden moss were flung hissing on the fire of the southern gap. Hold it for a quarter of an hour? I wished I had my armor.

✳ CHAPTER TEN ✳
ELEANOR: THE OUTLAWS

"Your foot," the Nightwalker lord said, and I looked at him blankly, not understanding. With a disgusted look, he seized me by the hips and heaved me up the side of the white horse. I tried to twist myself to land properly in the seat, but holding me half lying over the saddle with one hand, he grabbed my leg by the calf and shoved it across the horse's back. My skirts caught on the cantle of the saddle, and he muttered something that was probably Nightwalker cursing and untangled me, straightening my gown but hauling skirt and petticoats over my thighs. Then he adjusted the stirrups and stuck my feet into them as though I were a helpless child. I was mortified. I tugged at my skirts but could not get myself decently covered. Lord Romner made some joke about human women's legs, but he sounded annoyed at my helplessness. He put the reins into my hands, giving me instructions on where to go, what to do, which I hardly heard, I was so furious and ashamed. I knew I could not keep my seat above a trot at best, riding sideways without a proper sidesaddle or someone to hold on to me, but still, I felt shamed, with my legs exposed to those three men. Strange how such a minor thing can seem so important, even when life itself is at stake.

I was utterly unprepared for the horse's sudden leap into motion. So were the soldiers outside, thank Sypat. And on that white warlock horse, hidden by the scarlet cloak wrapped tightly around me and the hood pulled low, I suppose they thought

I was a dangerous Nightwalker warlock who had appeared out of nowhere and would shortly disappear again. I heard distant shouts. Someone was chasing me, but I could not look back to see how many.

I had never ridden a galloping horse, except for that furious dash to the ring of stones, when Korby was clutching me tightly, so that did not really count. Now all my attention was devoted to staying on. I didn't bother trying to guide the horse but clung to the saddle. Tree trunks flashed by; twigs whipped my legs and face. Part of the time I had my eyes shut.

In one of the brief moments I had them open, our path plunged down into a narrow valley, following a stream. Hemlocks grew thick on a north-facing slope that never saw much sun, and now, with twilight drawing near, it was dark and mysterious, a ballad forest where anything could happen. And when Sennanna thundered beneath those trees, the world changed. Suddenly I could see, but all color had leached from my vision. The world was misty and gray, and I could not feel the hemlock twigs that should have been flicking my face.

The white mare's wild gallop slowed to a trot, and I dared to gather up the slack in the reins. My heart pounded. The sound of the brook running beside us was muffled. Sennanna pushed through sapling hemlocks and ferns that seemed strangely insubstantial, though she had to go around the older trees, and when I stretched out a curious hand their ghost-gray bark was rough under my fingers. The mare waded the stream and took us up out of the valley, heading north again.

The halfworld. The horse had carried me into the Nightwalkers' halfworld.

The forest was silent, all gray and black, but curiously light. Stars were already burning like white torches in an ink-black sky. I wondered if this was how owls and cats saw the world. I was certain it was past time for camp and fires and supper. Just when I was beginning to wonder if I would be trapped in the halfworld until I encountered another Nightwalker, the world became suddenly darker, heavy and velvet around me. The shadows were merging into true night and what sky I could see was red with the last of the sunset. We were back in the familiar forest.

Fear returned too. In the halfworld, it had been possible not to worry, suspended in a dream. Now I could not escape what I understood. Maurey and Korby had been waiting for the shadows to grow deep with evening. They had sent me away and stayed behind, waiting until they could enter the halfworld, but they had not expected to survive that long. If they had thought we could really hold out in the ring of stones, they would have kept me safe with them.

They were captive or dead. Sawfield would kill them, kill them horribly. Suddenly it was real, what they did to Nightwalkers. I could hardly bear to think of it, but I could not shake the thought from my mind. Maurey with his shy smile, laughing with Korby as if they were brothers. Lord Romner, who saw at once what needed to be done and did it, even while the three men jested together, their banter as lighthearted as if they had all the time in the world. No, I could not believe it. Surely they had escaped. The way Korby and the big gray stallion had fought, there in the gateway of the ring, he could not have been defeated, not by Sawfield himself. And Prince Maurey was a warlock.

I could not convince myself they could survive. A horrible cold sickness settled in my stomach, but I was not going to howl. The Rose Maiden would not weep and wail, not now, not yet. The Rose Maiden never gave up. I had to trust them, keep faith with them, by going on and finding Dunmorran safety, Dunmorran help. I prayed as I rode, not to Huvehla, but to Anaskto and to Mayn the Lady, protector of women, and to the Yerku, the twins who watched over warriors.

The white mare, Sennanna, slowed to a walk. She needed to rest more than I did. Was it safe to stop? I could not decide. When she hesitated, I urged her on. She tossed her head unhappily and obeyed, but not much farther on she halted again.

Perhaps she was right. The darkness was too thick to see my way. I did not want her to stumble over a root and injure herself. Something loomed up before my face, and I yelped and ducked. Only a branch. If we had still been trotting, it would have struck my head before I had time to avoid it.

"Very well, Sennanna, we shall stop," I said aloud, "and you are to behave yourself and be a good horse and not run away."

Talking to a horse. Katerina would laugh at me...I was trying very hard not to think about Katerina as I had last seen her, shouting at me while riding in Sawfield's lap, shouting hatred at the men I thought had become friends to both of us. What on earth had possessed her to act so madly, even if she did believe all the winter tales of predatory warlocks? How could she truly believe I would give myself to Baron Sawfield? I doubted he was the sort of man who would wait for my father's permission, however forced, and a wedding. He would want to make sure of me, so that Dugald could not claim me. My stomach heaved, and I leaned over only just in time to avoid being sick all over myself and poor Sennanna. Huvehla—Anaskto, help me. I needed to rein in my treacherous imagination, to stop thinking of such things: of execution pyres and men dying in gory battle and Sawfield's bloody hands on me. If I could not be strong now, then when?

The Rose Maiden, I decided, could fend for herself in the forest, like any errant knight of ballad. She would. Starting now.

Awkwardly, I swung my leg over and slid down Sennanna's side. My knees felt like they were filled with jelly, and I only stayed upright by clinging to the harness. The mare turned her head and nuzzled my hair. Her breath was warm and oddly sweet, comforting.

"Come along, my lady," I said. "Let's at least find some water."

I led her along the path, listening for the sound of trickling water, and when the ground began to dip I turned aside and followed the slope downwards, nearly blind, feeling my way through clawing branches and grabbing roots, until my foot squished. It was black night now. I could not hear water, but Sennanna snorted and pushed past me, mud sucking at her hooves. She was a vague white blur, slurping water. I stumbled over ferny hummocks, trying vainly to keep my feet dry, and felt around until I had the reins again. We seemed to have found a small pool. I drank just as greedily as the horse, after rinsing out my mouth.

I did not let her drink her fill—I had an idea that might not be a good thing, though I did not know whether horses, like humans, got belly cramps from too much cold water. I tugged her to higher ground and felt around the Nightwalker's saddlebags until I found what seemed to be a length of rope. This I tied around the horse's neck, tethering her to a tree, before I began fumbling with buckles, trying to take her bridle off. I managed in the end. I left the saddle. I did not think I could get it back on.

"I'm sorry," I told her, certain she was giving me disapproving looks in the darkness. "That's the best I can do." Korby and Prince Maurey always groomed the horses before they did anything about their own supper, and I felt very guilty for not trying to do the same, but it was dark and I was exhausted and near-hopeless and simply trying to think about what to do made me suddenly feel like weeping.

Stop that, I told myself. What I needed was food to give me strength and rest so I could go on in the morning. That was sensible and practical. Deal with the essentials, do not worry about the rest. The horse was ripping at plants, though I could not see what she was eating. Nothing bad for horses, I hoped.

I had found a sack of what felt like grain while I was looking for rope, so I poured a heap of this out on the ground in front of Sennanna. I had also found some sort of sticky slablike cake wrapped in waxed cloth. When I broke off a piece to nibble, it tasted of nuts and fruit and honey, as well as spices, like the feast-day cakes my father's bakers made in Desmin-month for the solstice and the death and rebirth of Phaydos. I discovered that despite everything I was as ravenous as the horse. I ate a big chunk of cake without searching for any other food.

Even if I had been able to see what I was doing, I would not have made a fire. I feared Baron Sawfield more than wolves or bears or lynxes.

I fell asleep huddled against the bole of a tree, wrapped in a warm cloak that smelt of a stranger.

I woke before dawn, when the birds began carolling. My hair and the red cloak were covered with dew, and the white mare stood at the length of her tether, gazing down towards the boggy pool. We both had a good drink and some breakfast—more sticky cake for me—and then I had to decide how to go on. I was not even certain which way I should be going. I did not clearly remember the directions the Nightwalker lord had given me and I had no idea if the path the horse had followed last night had even been going in the right direction. Still, I supposed that if I went more or less north, I should eventually strike the main track to Greyrock Town, where the king was supposed to be. And if…if Prince Maurey and Korby had escaped and were following me, they would know where I was going and would catch up, somehow. If they had not…

I did not have time to waste. North it was.

I managed to bridle Sennanna and, with more difficulty, get my knots undone to put the rope away. The mare nosed at me impatiently, and I stroked her cheek. Her affection made me feel a bit warmer inside; even the comfort of a dumb beast is better than being alone and hopeless. And even dirty, covered with mud and twigs, burrs in her tail, she was truly the most beautiful horse I had ever seen. Her muzzle and ears and legs were charcoal-gray, her coat should have been pearly white, and her eyes were large and black. She was graceful and delicate as a deer, tall and lean, and I had no idea how I was going to get myself back in the saddle.

My skirts and petticoats caught on scrubby bushes and saplings as I led Sennanna up the slope we had trampled down the night before. When I tried to stride out boldly along the path, walking confidently as the Rose Maiden should, leading the tall proud horse, my skirts wrapped themselves around my legs, hobbling me.

I stopped. I had seen—yes, there it was, a little knife in a sheath fastened to the harness. I took it, with Sennanna tugging at the reins as though she understood we had to keep moving, and I ripped the skirt of my gown and my layers of petticoats, front and back, from above my knees down to the hem. Now I could ride astride and not look so indecent—if I could ever climb to the saddle.

The great gnarled foot of a beech tree helped, providing a mounting-block so I could get my foot in the stirrup, and then there I was, atop the horse, all by myself. Sennanna tossed her head, as if she too felt that at last things were being done properly, and set out at a trot. About the middle of the morning, when our path crossed another that I thought led more directly north, I tried to turn her aside. She flattened her ears, lowered her head stubbornly and refused to move until I let her go as she wanted. That was when I remembered Romner putting some sort of spell on her to guide us.

And that was how I traveled for several days, although after that first night, I did figure out how to unsaddle the poor horse, and, even greater triumph (after the first unsuccessful attempt), how to get all her gear back on her in the morning, so that neither it nor I fell off.

I never dared to make a fire, afraid of what it might attract, so I lived on cake, biscuits and dried fruit, though the Nightwalker had a good supply of cracked wheat, dried meat and something tough and purple I eventually concluded was seaweed, though whether it was for him or the horse I did not know. I felt great relief on the afternoon that our path merged with a broad well-used track running northwesterly. It was churned up with the passage of many horses, and Sennanna turned onto it without protest, breaking into a smooth joyous canter when I gave her a touch of my heels. It was not exactly civilization—the trees were massive spreading things, some big around as Aunt Nan's little cabin, their branches, thick as trees themselves, shutting out the sky—but after so long alone, it felt like it.

That evening, though, Sennanna took me off the track, onto a narrow path that wound and climbed a stony ridge, pushing through tangles of cedar and velvet-pronged sumac.

"This had better be a shortcut," I told her. "If you get us lost, my lady, I'll have to have words with your master."

She flicked her ears and snorted, lowering her head for the climb. I slid down to lead her, as the way became steeper yet. Near the top of the ridge we found a spring bubbling cold from between a mossy crack in the rocks, so I let Sennanna drink and filled Lord Romner's leather water-bottle. It was time to think about making camp, before it became too dark to see, but I wanted to reach the high ground, where neither the horse nor I would fall over this near-cliff in the night. While I was kneeling at the spring, I smelled smoke and something so delicious my mouth started watering. For a moment I could not identify it.

Roasting meat?

Sennanna stamped a foot, snuffing the air. Then a dog began to bay, a belling cry that started off as puppyish yapping and turned into full-throated howling—abruptly silenced.

Time to get out of here. I resumed my scramble up the ridge, now almost on hands and knees, with Sennanna nearly treading on me. No sooner had I reached the top and straightened up, wiping mud from my hands and looking around for the path, when a voice said, "Step away from the horse, if you know what's good for you."

I looked around. A figure, a boy no taller than me, seemed to solidify out of the trees. He was tanned brown, his disheveled, roughly cropped hair was light brown, his scarf and smock and hose were dyed brown and muddy green, and he was as hard to see as a motionless partridge. He had a bow drawn, the arrow aimed unwaveringly at me.

I dropped the reins and stepped away from Sennanna, my heart pounding.

"It's all right," I began to say, "I'm not—" But even a fool could see I was not a Nightwalker, and this boy did not look a fool. A girl about the same age emerged from the trees. She wore a peasant's short-skirted gown, its draggled hem at mid-calf, and a black-and-gray-chequered shawl hiding her hair, as well camouflaged as the boy. The girl took the mare's reins, making soothing shushing noises when the horse blew at her and sidled a nervous step away. She carried a quarterstaff.

The dog started to yelp and then howl again.

"I told you not to take that damned dog," the boy snapped. "It's going to be nothing but trouble."

The girl hunched her shoulders, her face tight and pinched and gray around the eyes, going even more miserable. "She's just a puppy. She'll learn."

"And while she's learning she'll be yelling at everyone who comes within a quarter mile of us. Oh, go on, Fu. Give me the reins, this one isn't any threat." And with that insulting remark, the boy slacked off his bow, returned the arrow to the quiver on his back and took the reins. She must be his sister, I thought; they shared the same square high-cheekboned face and the same bluebell-colored eyes. The girl ran, bare feet making no noise at all, away through the trees, and I heard her voice, suddenly stern, saying, "No! Bad! Quiet!"

The howling became a muffled whine, as though some puppy's muzzle was being held shut.

"This way," said the boy, and he led Sennanna in the girl's wake, crossing the path that was likely supposed to be my shortcut. Now the mare decided not to argue. Probably she felt it was time to camp. Wretched thing. I had no choice but to follow. The boy was barefoot too. He turned to scowl back at me every few steps.

We waded an icy stream just too wide to jump and came to the base of another ridge, more of a cliff, dark with cedars. The stream tumbled down it in noisy white thunder. The boy tied Sennanna to a maple sapling and took my elbow, half leading, half dragging me onwards. The girl was on her knees by a fire at the narrow mouth of a cave. Her shawl had slipped back, showing a long braid of silver-blond hair. She cuddled a half-grown pup on her lap, while using a long knife to prod at a fowl of some sort roasting on a stick over the fire. Pheasant? My mouth watered again.

"It's just about done, Robin," she said.

"Watch the girl while I see what's in the saddlebags," Robin said. He still sounded angry, though the puppy scrambled from the sister's lap, prancing to meet him, and he stooped to rub its ears. The blue-roan coat, mottled with solid black patches, was very distinctive; it was a hare-hunting bluehound of the breed

King Dugald was so fond of, not a peasant's dog. It was tied up, and its collar and long leash were fine red-dyed leather. I opened my mouth to accuse them of stealing some nobleman's dog, and then shut it again. There were a number of stupid things I could have said, and that was probably one of them. Better to stay silent.

The girl and I looked at one another while Robin, silent as some forest spirit, unsaddled Sennanna, with a few twists and a knot fashioning a halter from the rope I had been tying around her neck at night. I resolved to learn how to do that. Maybe I could even get him to teach me. He could not be too wicked a person; he began grooming the horse with a knot of grass, ignoring the saddlebags. I was distracted from the boy when the girl rose, the knife still in her hand. The puppy ambled over to sniff my boots, and the girl studied me just as carefully.

"I'm Fuallia," she said after a moment, and added carefully, "my brother is Robin."

"Not Jock Wildwood?" I asked. Jock Wildwood was either a legendary outlaw or a Lesser Power of the Westwood, depending on what you believed. The peasants danced on the first of Fuallin led by a youth and maiden dressed as Jock Wildwood and his Fuallin-Queen.

Fuallia merely shrugged. Maybe she heard too many jokes about her name. She was probably only a year or two younger than I was, but her eyes looked old and weary, and her face was almost gaunt.

I thought of trying to run, but she had that knife, and I did not think I could outrun her, let alone an arrow from Robin.

"You might as well sit down," she said. "Who are you?"

"Where did you steal the horse?" demanded her brother, returning with the bag of cracked wheat and the jerky, the last bit of the cake and what looked suspiciously like the purse of coin I had found at the bottom of one saddlebag.

"I didn't," I said. "It was lent to me."

"Of course it was," he said. "You know what they'll do to you for robbing a Talverdine courier?"

"Do you know what they'll do to you for—?" I stopped. Robin's face was as bleak and weary as his sister's, and now I recognized what ailed them. I had seen the same face in my own mirror. Some heavy sorrow was haunting them, devouring rest and peace of mind.

"Can I help?" I found myself asking, foolishly.

Fuallia, cuddling the puppy again, looked up, eyes wide and startled. Robin gave me a long cold stare. "What makes you think we need a beggar-brat's help?" he asked. He shook the purse. It jingled musically, and he smiled slightly and handed it to Fuallia. She stowed it away inside the neck of her gown without a word. "What do you think we can get for a Nightwalker mare?"

Fuallia shook her head. "It's too dangerous. We'd better just let her go."

"There's a good many knights would pay well to tuck her away in some out-of-sight meadow, to breed colts from their chargers," Robin said, meaning Sennanna, not me. I think he was trying to persuade himself as much as his sister.

"Someone will be looking for the horse," Fuallia said. "They'd find us. You can't hide us from warlocks the way you did from those men-at-arms this morning."

"Look," I said. "Let me go. I'm a minstrel, carrying an urgent message to Greyrock Castle. Keep the purse, I don't need it, but let me take the horse and go."

"A minstrel, is it? Maybe I missed seeing your harp? Your lute?"

"I play flutes," I said and then remembered my flutes were with Maurey and Korby, if they were even…Powers be with them.

The corner of Robin's mouth rose; it was a sneer, not a smile. "Of course."

"Have you heard of the Rose Maiden?" I persisted. "I could sing for you."

"Haven't. Don't want to."

"Let her go, Robin," Fuallia said with a sigh, as if the argument was too much for her. She lifted the bird off the fire, set it on a wooden dish and began carving it neatly. Robin, without being asked, went into the cave and came back with a flat round loaf of bread and a basket of radishes. He grabbed the puppy away from the meat and sat on its leash.

"You already had the giblets, Taddie," he said sternly, but when the puppy whined he gave her a piece of crackling golden skin.

"You'll upset her belly," Fuallia said, and handed me a third of the bread, heaped with slices of roast pheasant, and passed the radishes as politely as if we were sitting at her table. "We have wine," she added, and the two looked at one another.

"Sure," said Robin. "It's a special occasion." He went back to the cave, returning with a sealed jar and earthenware cups, pale green patterned with acorns, fine enough for a knight's table.

"Ah," I said, "Jock Wildwood and Fuallin-Queen always provide a noble feast for their victims."

For the first time, Robin actually smiled. It made his face look quite nice. "Before they surrender them for a mighty ransom."

"If I'm just a beggar-brat, who are you planning to ransom me to?"

"The forest's crawling with lords and ladies this summer," Robin said lightly. "I'm sure some of them will be interested in a beggar's brat who pinched a Nightwalker horse."

I snorted disdainfully but said nothing more. He was all too right. I could only hope he chose to send word of me to

Greyrock Town and that Baron Sawfield did not stumble across this cosy little den of outlaws first.

Robin filled a pitcher with water straight from the waterfall and mixed wine and water for each of us. I was quite certain there was very little water going into mine, even before I tasted it. They meant to make me sleepy with wine, so that I would give them no trouble. And perhaps when I woke up, they, and Sennanna, would be long gone and far away. I did not imagine it would take them more than a few minutes to pack up whatever possessions they kept in the cave and disappear for good. Although they might get a surprise, when Lord Romner's spell began pushing Sennanna to head for Greyrock Town in the morning. I smiled and sipped the wine. Hardly any water at all.

The pheasant was delicious. I wrapped Lord Romner's red cloak more tightly around me and managed to keep dribbling wine on it whenever they were not watching. I was going to stink like a drunkard before the evening was over.

"So," I said, "you're outlaws."

"Jock Wildwood and Fuallin-Queen," chuckled Robin. Maybe he had not put that much water in his own wine.

"What did you do? Why are you outlawed?"

"Killed a man," Robin said, looking at the fire and giving Taddie the hound the last piece of his bread and pheasant. I was not sure I believed him. He might have been trying to scare me. I spilled some more wine on my cloak and held out my cup for Fuallia to refill. She did not bother with water at all this time. The look she gave me was strange: cold and remote and sad. I had a surge of sick fear that Robin might be planning to murder me and that Fuallia knew it. But I looked at them again and could not believe it. They were so young.

I wanted to write a song about them, to spin some romantic tragic story to explain why they were alone in the forest, driven from their home. I wanted to write them a happy ending. Perhaps I had swallowed more of the wine than I had intended. I was more careful with the second cup.

The shadows crept around us, thickening into night. The puppy yawned and crawled into Fuallia's lap. Fuallia yawned. *Sleep,* I wished them. *Mayn, lady of night, send them sleep.* I let my own head sink forward, cup tipping. Then I sat up, yawned.

"Does Jock Wildwood give his guests a feather bed too?" I asked, slurring my words together.

Fuallia waved her hand. "Inside," she said and got to her feet.

It was too dark to see a thing inside the cave, but Fuallia guided me to a heap of bracken and fir boughs by feel. I did not even take my boots off, and Fuallia, with the puppy, curled up beside me, as Katerina so often had. I kept my eyes open, staring into nothing, afraid that if I let them close, sleep would take me. Robin did not join us right away. I hoped he was taking Sennanna to the stream for a drink. I hoped he was not really going to murder me.

I hoped he would hurry up and get to his bed before I fell asleep. The waterfall was a musical roar, carrying me away.

I kept my breathing slow and even, and pinched my thigh every time I felt my eyelids start to flutter. Robin came into the cave, treading softly. He moved like a cat. Like Korby, I thought. He reminded me of Korby, for all he was so small and delicate compared to the big Fenlander. He had the same careful confident way of moving—a fighter, a dancer, something like that. The same way of watching the world, as if a little removed from it all, as if he saw things no one else was seeing. I pinched myself again. I had been asleep after all. I could hear Fuallia breathing beside me, and Robin in the same heap of bracken, on the other side of her. That did not seem quite decent, but

I supposed the cave was not very big and everyone was fully clothed. Was the boy asleep? That was the question. I waited, listening. The puppy smacked her lips, dreaming of food. Nothing else stirred.

I sat up, slowly. If anyone woke I would say I had to go the bushes again. On my hands and knees, I crept out of the cave. The night was black, not a glimmer escaping the banked fire. I felt my way cautiously to where I had last seen Sennanna. She was still there, a pale hint of shape. She rumbled a greeting and lipped at my hands.

I stumbled around in the dark, groping and finding roots, trees, thorns and a pile of horse dung before I chanced on the saddle and bridle. Saddling the mare in the darkness was a nightmare. Leather creaked, buckles clattered, and I had to keep reminding myself that the waterfall would muffle all such noise, or I would have panicked and become even clumsier. Finally the job was done.

"I know you need to rest, Sennanna, my dear," I whispered to her, "but we need to get away from the outlaws. So could you please do your magic trick and take us out of here?" I started to lead her back the way we had come, towards that twisty little path along the top of the lower ridge. I kept my hand on her neck. I was unsure how the halfworld magic worked, and the last thing I needed was for the horse to disappear and leave me behind.

As I had hoped, Sennanna did not like walking in the black dark anymore than I did. Between one step and the next, the night around me changed, and in the dim gray—dimmer and darker than the daytime halfworld—I could see again. I sighed with relief. "Good girl." Before long we found a fallen log I could use to get into the saddle.

I could not get the outlaws out of my mind, especially Fuallia, cuddling the stolen dog as if holding it eased some ache too deep for healing. I found tears trickling down my cheeks and sniffed, wiping my face. Foolish. They had meant to hold me captive and ransom me, and what were the odds but that the first person they found willing to pay was Baron Sawfield? They might have sold me to him. But still, I wished I knew their story.

Hour after hour passed, and we were back on what I hoped was the main Greyrock track, far from the outlaws' cave. My head nodded, my eyes blurred, and I was nearly asleep in the saddle. Sennanna plodded, her head hanging. We had to stop. We were still in the halfworld—could we sleep away the daylight hours there, hidden from any pursuers? And how did I tell the horse that was what I wanted?

Suddenly she pricked her ears, raised her head and then, to my horror, whinnied, stepping out of the halfworld into golden morning as she did so.

Another horse answered. Sennanna broke into a scuffling trot, so unlike her usual proud floating gait, but I was so used to letting her have her head that I did not try to slow her, even for her own good.

An armed man on horseback was riding to meet us as we rounded a bend, horn raised to his lips, about to sound a warning. He lowered it unblown, frowning. I did rein in, for one panicked moment about to wheel Sennanna and flee, but then the soldier's livery sunk into my head—his surcoat was blue, with a black tower on it, outlined in silver rays: the royal arms of Dunmorra. A sentry in such arms on the road could mean only one thing: I had found King Dugald's expedition to Greyrock Town.

"Madam?" he asked. I suspect he wanted to sound stern and suspicious, but he looked more puzzled than anything. "Your name and business on this road?"

"Eleanor of Eswy," I said, as regal as I could be, trying not to cringe and hunch apologetically, trying to look him in the eye. I was the Rose Maiden. I was…I was this man's future queen, and I needed to begin as I meant to go on. No cringing. "Eleanor, Crown Princess of Eswy. Take me to the king."

The soldier frowned but gestured me forward and turned his horse again to fall in at my side. A sentry. He escorted me only so far as another mounted man-at-arms, murmured softly in his ear and then, as I thanked him, saluted me, wheeling his horse to return to his post. Watching for outlaws, I wondered? Had Robin and Fuallia actually robbed the *king's* camp the night before I met them? And how, with all these sentries and dogs about?

There had been tents pitched among the trees, but they were being packed up onto a string of sturdy mules now. Armed men and serving-folk were busy around their horses. Several dogs, bluehounds and one big, shaggy, piebald beast like a long-haired mastiff, wandered about, nosing into things or watching lazily. Three bluehound puppies were being walked on leashes by a worried-looking boy.

A crowd of men and women opened up as I approached. There were men-at-arms, knights, ladies, serving-folk, a dozen scruffy men in leather and plaid blankets and long braids like Korby—I realized later a few of those were women, though it was very hard to tell. An old man who looked like a clerk frowned. A young one who might have been a lord hid a burst of laughter behind his hand. A woman with curling red-gold hair and a most outlandish costume of embroidered long tunic and green barbarian trousers stared, her head to one side, a look of worry tilting delicate red-gold brows. Even then, I felt a pang. She was so beautiful, and she was standing so familiarly next to—next to the king. My betrothed husband. I knew him not by his looks, which were pleasant and ordinary—brown hair, brown beard, blue eyes—or by his plain blue doublet and hose, with a black leather jerkin such as any gentleman might wear, but by the way he was the center of them all. And he had a look of his brother too, somehow. Something about the eyes, different in color though they were.

The king recognized me too. I didn't know then that Lovell had sent him that sketch he had drawn last winter. If I had known, it would have made no difference. *Dugald knew me.* He strode towards me, me in my ripped, filthy, ugly gown, filthy hair, all rats'-nests and twigs, and as I swung my leg over and more or less fell down Sennanna's side he caught me in his arms.

"Eleanor!" he said, as if I was the most astonishing, most wonderful thing in the world. "My dear lady!"

So the pawn had eluded all the dangers, crossed the game-board through great perils and reached the safety of the far side of the board, where she could be acknowledged a queen. This was no game, though, and the sacrificed pieces were not scattered on the table waiting for the next match. I felt as guilty as if I had betrayed Prince Maurey and Korby and Lord Romner myself, when I had to tell King Dugald they had been left behind several days before, besieged and outnumbered. But he did not blame me; he held me the tighter.

It seemed perfectly natural and decent to lean my head on his chest, to feel his arms fold tight around me, to feel his breath stir my hair. It felt like coming home.

✤ CHAPTER ELEVEN ✤
KORBY: WILD FIRE

"Move stones?" Romner asked. "How?"

"You remember the song about the Makers walking the stones to build the Senna Causeway? It should be possible with the right words," Maurey told him. "It's in the song itself. Translate it back into the older speech, and you'll see how it should go. You take the north, I'll do the west."

"Easy for you to say," Romner grumbled.

Sawfield's men charged. They were smarter this time, not coming in a mob that would hamper their own movements. Two came at me, one from each side. They wanted to keep me pinned there while others put the fires out and got in behind us.

Two voices sang in Talverdine, not together, each keeping its own time. The song dropped low, then rose, high and sharp. Power rang in it. I'd never felt a Nightwalker spell-working like that one. Romner sounded strained, desperate, like a man struggling to lift something well beyond his weight. Maurey had gone remote and cold, the way he did, so that there was nothing to him but the task in hand, as though he became nothing but a tool for the power. The strange thing was, I could feel the whole circle changing. A…sound, for lack of a better word, that I hadn't known was there shifted, the way the note of a tiny stream will shift as you move the stones over which it flows. Whatever they were doing was changing the nature of the ring, though they didn't intend it and didn't have the ears to hear.

What they intended was impressive enough. I didn't see it myself, being otherwise occupied, but I swear what my lord says is true. In his song, he caught a stone from the next ring below and walked it, twisting and grinding through the moss, into the western gap. Men shouted and screamed and ran in terror as it moved, and with what attention I could spare I fanned that terror, feeding it, urging it into the panic that makes a man run blind and mindless.

"They're coming in the east!" Romner shouted, breaking his song.

One of my men was dead and the other stood off, panting, hesitating. I spared a glance behind. Maurey stumbled away from the gap and fell, pulled himself up and ran, sword drawn, to the east, hit the men crowding in there with a crash of steel and renewed flame—dry moss burns very well—and he flung the heat of the fires at the gap to dry and kindle the moss, but more was tossed on, hissing, and the fire sank again as a new onslaught of men rushed through. Maurey disappeared, borne down beneath them. Romner's voice cracked, and he fell to his knees, but a tall stone heaved itself into the north gap. He lurched up, cursing human half-breeds who didn't have the sense to know what was and wasn't possible, and ran to Maurey even as I shouted his name.

Two fresh horsemen engaged me, and I could do nothing for my lord. Their onrush forced us back. One had lost his helmet. I split his skull, and his horse bolted past into the ring, the corpse still in the saddle. Harrier squealed and reared, striking at a third man before us. Another horse crashed into us, and I lost the gateway entirely. We were all within the ring: men afoot who had taken the east, and the mounted men who had driven me from the south. Maurey was on his feet, back to back with Romner. The fools should call Boots, snorting and stamping among the trees, but the prince was probably too out of breath to whistle.

The fires were dying; all the trees within the ring were charred black spikes. Maurey got his back against one of the dead trunks, Romner before him, guarding the prince as he sang, his voice faint. Stone lurched, reluctantly, and dragged itself into the eastern gap, cutting off the rest of the men who had come up the east, but since I had lost the south it did no good; we could not hold the ring. The shadows stretched, dark and reaching towards evening. Dark enough? Maurey found the breath to call Boots. A brown stray followed, and Romner grabbed it, so we had height again, though the stubs of the burnt trees still crowded us, hampering the horses. The men afoot backed warily away, not a single one with polearms of any sort, at a serious disadvantage against mounted men. I rode them down in turning back to the southern gap, where more horsemen were coming. Sawfield himself was among those, coming to collect his prize, who the Yerku send was a few miles away by now. If Maurey and Romner could deal with the ones still in the ring…

But Harrier and I were both faltering, and a thrust I was too slow to block bit between the horn plates of my brigandine, bit between ribs. I didn't lose my sword, but the world went dim and roaring and slow as I bled over Harrier. I parried clumsily, and Harrier, knowing something wrong, wheeled away from the press of bodies, losing the gap again. I started to fall, everything growing dark. Dark enough? It was only my eyes.

"Korby!" Maurey caught me, holding me upright by a shoulder, Boots jostling close, and I blinked some sense back into my head.

"Kill the warlock!" Katerina screeched at Sawfield from some safe distance. "Save the princess!"

Sawfield and the half-dozen of his guard, who had till now only watched, charged us, confident, exulting already in their victory.

The man who had wounded me closed in again, and the leading riders of Sawfield's guard were at the gap, grinning. I pulled away from Maurey. I could at least finish off the nearest, I thought blurrily; he'd have to take the others. Romner was riding to us...I was between the newcomers and Maurey, and they wanted it that way. They made for me—the one who'd killed too many of them—their hate overriding any sensible fear of warlocks. The prince spun Boots around us, sweeping the man I was failing to fight aside, and it seemed like lightning arced from his sword to the blade of the leading rider. The air grew sharp and harsh in my throat, snapping on metal, on sword edges and buckles, hissing on mail. They should have run then. Maurey was blade to blade with a soldier nearly mad with terror, when the wild lightning broke like a curtain of rain away from him, tearing the air. Maurey shouted in despair, words stumbling to assemble some spell of protection. I had just sense and strength enough to draw the safety of the earth over us, me and Maurey and Romner and our horses together. It worked. I felt the wild fire seeking us, hungry, but it could not bite. Boots nevertheless screamed and tried to bolt from the sheet of lighting that crashed and washed over the stones of the ring like violent ripples in a puddle, touching us like water, nothing worse. It killed the rest, men and horses. The men fortunate enough to be still in the gap fled, and the stones drank the lightning, stilling it.

I did fall then, but the prince was there to catch me. I could feel him shaking, kneeling on the blackened earth, holding my head.

"Romner!" he shouted, fear in his voice, and Romner answered, "Still alive," leading over the horse that had thrown him in its panic.

Sunset, and the shadows stretched over us.

"*Now* it gets dark," Romner muttered. He pulled us, horses

and all, into the halfworld, where it was safe for me to give up
and simply faint.

I was wrapped in heavy smothering fog. Sometimes the prince
and Lord Romner were there, moving around, and I knew
Romner must have worked his spell that could hold a human or
a normal animal in the halfworld without a Nightwalker's touch.
Sometimes I was alone, and everything was dark, streaked and
flashing with sheets of silent white lightning.

I worried about Eleanor and sought after her, feared her run
down by Sawfield and those who had fled, slain in revenge for all
the deaths we had caused. I saw her, sometimes, riding beneath
the trees. She was dressed in rags, a troll's cloak of human hair,
woven of her own braids, flying behind her. That was a nightmare,
probably, but I did see her. I saw her again, wearing blue velvet,
her hair clean and smooth, touched with gold in the light of a
campfire and loose over her shoulders. She was surrounded by
vague dark figures I could not see but knew to be friends. At least
two of them shivered with a touch of witchery, and I felt the tug of
blood, knew them to be my own, Fen-witches and Moss'avvers—
Mollie and Tam. Probably they were traveling with my cousin
Oakhold, which meant they were on their way to Greyrock Town
with the king. I couldn't seem to pull myself together enough to
creep into their dreams and demand to know if the girl was safe,
if the king was safe, if we were at war with Eswy yet. Demand to
know if I was safe, or if for my sins I was a wandering shade.

I could see Sawfield and the tattered ruins of his band riding
south for the border, to get themselves safely over into Eswy, out of
Dunmorra before the vengeance of Dugald and the Nightwalkers
could overtake them. Katerina rode with them, alone, ignored
and weeping.

I saw Eleanor again, still in rags but a human woman, not a
witch-troll this time. She sat unhappy and angry at another fire,

and a weak human witch sat beside her, hair like moonlight on snow, petting a dog. A girl walking the edge of darkness, that was how I saw the stranger, with little will left to force her way onwards. Another girl strode into the light, sharp and angry, fiercely protective of her silver-haired sister and roiling with witchery. She was someone who might give me a fair fight, mind to mind, if only she knew what she was doing. She held secrecy around them, around all that pocket of the forest. I reached to touch her, wanting to know what they did with the princess— but I had seen the princess with the king, had I not? Did the damned and outcast shade I had become wander between past and future as well? What were these two? They were no Fenlanders, not forest-folk, either. Any with the old blood in the Westwood had been slaughtered back in Conqueror Hallow's day. My gran had claimed there were still a few families in the mountains with the old blood, though; mountains felt right for these two, stark rock and high ice and secrets held under the open sky. The girl felt my touch and blazed up in anger and fear, not knowing what I was.

She flung me into another dream, or I pulled it from their memories, as I fell away.

The silver-haired girl ran towards the dark plume of smoke. She had been hunting hares on the mountainside and supper dangled from her hand. She dodged through the copse of pines that sheltered the cottage and the sheep-sheds and the two wind-bent apple trees. The hare dropped from her hand. The cottage was a bonfire, and as she watched the roof fell in with a roar and a fountain of sparks.

"Grandda!" she shouted and ran again, around the corner of a low sheep-shed.

Horses? Two strangers stood in what had been the dooryard, looking up the long narrow valley to where the peaks closed in, all ravines and scree and high snows. They turned, hearing her shriek, animal rage. The old man lay a little distance from them, all too plainly dead in a puddle of blood, an axe near his hand, and the dogs sprawled by him. He had kept both dogs home that morning when Robin went up to High End; he wanted them to help shift the Near Flock down lower…

Bow in her hand, quiver on her back. She had loosed an arrow and drawn her bow on another while they were still reaching for swords. The first took a man in the throat. The second flew awry and stuck in the other man's shoulder, slowed by heavy leather. They were only light-headed arrows for hare and pheasant. He wrenched it out and flung it away, but she advanced on him, speaking calmly, coldly, implacably—an invocation of the Powers in a tongue that was not quite Fen. Perhaps he took it for a curse. Perhaps he saw her as a manifestation of Fescor himself, who escorted the shades of the dead to Geneh. He abandoned his dying companion as she took aim again, scrambled to a horse and fled, the riderless second mount hard on his heels.

Air still gurgled in the first man's throat, but as she stood over him, it ceased. She fell to her knees, silent, and was still there when her sister, fallen sick and vision-wracked, came back from High End, having run herself to exhaustion, knowing what she would find.

"You've butchered sheep and hens; you're hunting all the time—what's the difference? No, I know he's a man and that's different, but anything fights to protect itself, its family. You did no more than anyone down in the village would have done; no one can blame you."

"I felt the life go out of him," the silver girl said. "I felt his thoughts stop."

"Oh, Fu."

"We have to get away from here. We can't go to the reeve and say we killed a man defending what's ours, killed the man who killed

Grandda. They'll say we brought it on ourselves; they'll say the Powers have cursed us, the way they did when Mama was ill and no one would come up to nurse her. They'll say we're bringing trouble on them down there in the village. This was a lord's man, maybe from the Warden at Greyrock, who knows. No one'll take our word against a lord. Stop crying, Fu. We don't have time. We'll bury Grandda and the dogs. The foxes can take the hens, and the sheep'll look out for themselves, they'll have to. The wolves might miss a few, and maybe we'll be back some day to find them. But for now we have to be gone before anyone comes looking. And if they do take us—you say it was me shot him, all right? Fu? Can you do that? Fu, it wasn't your fault, there wasn't anything else you could have done. Powers, why wasn't I here?"

The short-haired girl dragged the killer's body away, gracelessly by his heels. His arms trailed. His left palm was marked—tattooed. The girl noticed and so did I, seeing her memory. Concentric circles in black, lines joining one to the next.

The Yehillon.

Search him! I pleaded. Find what else he's carrying, find who he is, what he is? But she dumped him in a ditch out of sight and fetched a spade from the sheep-shed to begin digging her grandfather's grave. The silver girl, Fu, straightened the old man's body and smoothed the fur of the two dogs, and then just sat, her hands folded on her knees, looking inward.

Don't dwell on it, foolish child. It'll eat your heart out and leave you hollow. Your sister's right. What else could you have done? Get up and go on.

We needed to find this barren, narrow, mountain valley, which looked like a gash in a mountainside. We needed to find these mountain witch-girls, before someone did take them for unlawful killing or the assassin's friends hunted them down.

"Is he making sense yet?" the prince asked, kneeling to set a kettle of water on the fire by which I lay. It was daylight, and we were in a different part of the forest, with maples and ashes arching above us, willows making a silver-gray cloud over a brown stream.

"Yes," I said. "I always make sense."

"You say the strangest things in your sleep," Romner remarked, sounding interested but unconcerned, as if I were some antique curiosity. "Apparently you think we have to dig up a Yehillon, whatever that is."

"Why aren't we all dead?" Maurey asked.

I struggled to sit up and found myself lying down again, head whirling, his hand on my chest.

"Idiot," he said. "Stay put, and don't undo all our good work. We know why *you're* not dead at least, and it's entirely our doing, so remember to be nice to warlocks from now on. But why didn't I kill us all? I thought I had. I thought..."

"Hey." I put a hand over his, waiting for Romner to say something even ruder than usual about emotional Fenlanders, but he restrained himself. "You didn't."

"I lost control completely. We should have all died. Nothing I could do; I couldn't call it back. But you did something."

"Earth," I said and dug a hand, the only hand that seemed to answer, into the ground beside me by way of demonstration.

Ah. The other was bundled into a club of bandages. "Earth is greater than lightning. Earth can hold the lightning."

"So did those stones," Romner remarked. "There's old Making in that place, old, old magic. It's very like the Coronation Shrine up north of Dralla. I wonder what it was for?"

"Famous last stands," I suggested. "Eleanor's with the king, by the way."

"We gathered that, in the rare moments you spoke any intelligible language. But we couldn't make any sense out of, what was it? 'The scar on the mountain, that's what they want. It isn't the girls.'"

"What?" I frowned. "I don't remember that. But we need the girls anyhow, or we'll never find the valley that looks like someone sliced the mountainside with a knife."

"What valley, what girls?" Romner asked.

"Eleanor knows," I said. "Ask her when we get to Greyrock." And I drifted into sleep again. This time there were no dreams.

The next time I woke it was to a rosy sunset. We were camped under high and airy pines, and a shallow river leapt around rocks below a steep bank. I could smell fish roasting. The prince does not enjoy hunting, but show him a good deep lake or a swift river and all he can think about is fish. He and Romner were sketching things in the leaf mould and talking in quiet Talverdine.

"Harrier?" I asked.

"He's fine," said Maurey.

"In better shape than you, fortunately, because if we had to pair the little Eswyn horse with Boots to carry your litter, you would have slid into a ditch days ago."

"Where are we?"

"We should strike the Greyrock track tomorrow. Romner's going to ride on ahead in the morning and get someone to meet us with a wagon—they've been working on the last stretch of the road this spring, and Romner says it should be passable for carts, since it hasn't rained recently."

"I can ride."

"No, you can't. Don't be such a fool."

Romner snorted. "Stupid sheep-thief. We did not spend a night prying you from Fescor's loving embrace for you to kill yourself now."

"Sheep-thief? Romner, you like me. I never knew."

"Stop talking and let me get your head up so you can eat," my lord ordered, "before you fall asleep again."

Several weeks passed before I was on my feet again. I missed the meetings and the long discussions between Dugald and Queen Ancrena. She always looked at me a bit dubiously anyhow, as if I were some tame bear who'd broken my chain and was wandering loose, snuffling into things and shedding fur on the furniture. The upshot of all those meetings, though, was that my lord was appointed to be the new Warden of Greyrock, and a number of Talverdine knights and folk of House Keldyachi, the clan of Maurey's father, were appointed to remain in Greyrock as part of the garrison or to serve in Maurey's household.

I was cynical enough to wonder if Queen Ancrena meant all those pretty Nightwalker ladies to be part of her campaign to entice Maurey to marry a Nightwalker woman, preferably a Maker, as they called warlocks like his friend Aljess, who was captain of the new warden's guard. My cousin Oakhold came moping in to see me about it one day, shutting the door on the anteroom, where a couple of my lads were on duty. She dropped down on the floor with her back against my bed, her pale blue skirts, embroidered with red roses, spread out around her, her red-gold curls caught up in a net decorated with blue enamelled beads. Annot can manage to look elegant while roaming the hills in a sleet-storm looking for lost sheep, but she had almost entirely given up wearing tight-bodiced, full-skirted human women's gowns by that time.

"What's the special occasion?" I asked.

Annot didn't answer the question. "She still says no."

I couldn't see her face. She wouldn't be crying, not Annot. I didn't think so, anyway. But there was pain under her anger, both emotions still raw, for all she was used to them.

"Ancrena, you mean?"

"I don't see why he has to do what she says."

"Maurey? He doesn't," I said, "but having her blessing on your marriage matters to him, for your sake—your honor in Talverdin." In his own quiet way my lord could be as bloody-minded and bull-headed as the king. He was waiting for his aunt to admit a human was good enough for a Nightwalker prince.

"What about my honor in Dunmorra?" Annot muttered. She would never tell Maurey how much she was hurt by the things the old cats at court said. She would never tell anyone. She laughed and held her head high and let on she enjoyed being the wicked scandalous baroness, the Nightwalker prince's mistress. But we'd been children together; she knew there was no hiding such things from me. She knew too that I'd never betray her. She leaned her head back against the mattress, so I could see a little of her face. Not crying, but I'd have given the Nightwalker queen a piece of my mind if she had walked in just then.

"I used to think Queen Ancrena liked me."

"She does, but as a person. Not as her niece-by-marriage, and especially not as the mother of the children of the most powerful warlock born in who knows how many generations. They want Maurey to have lots of little Maker babies casting spells in their cradles, not red-haired poachers."

"Too bad I didn't get anything from my Moss'avver great-grandmama but orange hair. Perhaps a witch would be almost as good. Magic is magic."

"No, it isn't," I said, "and I'm pretty sure Her Grace wouldn't want me marrying Maurey either, if that's what you're suggesting."

She laughed.

"You could tell Maurey how you feel," I suggested.

"No. I'm not going to tell him he has to choose between his family and me. He lived so long without any family at all. And you're not to go dropping any of your un-subtle hints, either."

I gave her a lazy salute.

She snorted and scrambled to her feet. "So what do you think of the dress? I'm to be Eleanor's chief witness for the wedding."

"It's got straw all over it. Tam was just in from the stables telling me how much Harrier and Boots miss me and he didn't wipe his feet. I hope it's only straw."

She shrieked and whirled, trying to look at her rump. When I laughed, she rapped me on the head with a knuckle. "I don't care if you've grown up to be taller than me. You're still a horrible brat."

"Don't do that. I'm an invalid. The gown looks good, Annot."

"Every woman and man from Greyrock Town with any needle skill has been hired, and we've been plundering everyone's wardrobe, even the Nightwalkers', for silk and brocade to remake. Dugald is determined this is not going to look like some runaway match and Eleanor is not going to look like she came to him a beggar. You should see the pearls Ancrena gave her."

"I have."

"Are they going to be happy, do you think?" Annot asked. "Dugald deserves some happiness."

"So does Eleanor. Yes, I think so. They didn't have to marry.

He would have given her sanctuary in Dunmorra anyway, if they'd found they couldn't stand one another."

"Marriage should be more than just being able to stand one another."

"It would take an army to pry them apart. Trust me."

"Are you going to be on your feet for the wedding?"

"There's still a couple of weeks, and the physician let me totter as far as the window this morning." The sooner I was up, the sooner I could ride out looking for a high valley like a knife-gash in the mountains. Dugald had sent soldiers looking for Eleanor's outlaws, but they would not be found. I was certain of that. Queen Ancrena would have to do with a gift of only three bluehound puppies.

"All the way to the window? Does that mean yes, you will be at the wedding?"

"Can I be your escort and lean on you?"

"No, that's Maurey's job. You'll have to find some other woman to prop you up: a bigger one. If you leaned on me, we'd both fall over."

"Arrity Cook," I suggested, and young Alun opened the door just then to announce my lord, who came in with Aljess trailing him as bodyguard, wanting to know what we were laughing about.

✣ Chapter Thirteen ✣
Eleanor: Queen Consort

E ven before Lovell died, my marriage had been a move in a chess match my father played against his barons and his wife. Now, it was more than a tactic in a game, however serious. It was a weapon I could use against the people who had wanted to use me. I was blessed in that it could also make me, and let me make Dugald, very happy.

I felt I had known him forever.

There was no marriage treaty. Lovell's death made the agreement that my father had reached with Dugald the year before empty. Everything changed, now that I was heir. All we had was the letter my father had sent, pleading with Dugald to come to Eswy and marry me without delay. In that, he proposed to abdicate in favor of Dugald and me as joint monarchs of both realms. In effect, he suggested that Dunmorra and Eswy become one kingdom again, under one crown shared between husband and wife. This would not be easy. Dugald had his council, which gave much weight to the representatives of the barons, the university, the sisterhood of Mayn and even the common folk of the kingdom, while my father had his council of barons, who gave little weight to what he or the common folk wanted. We both agreed that a united crown was something to strive for, though, and we wrote a declaration saying so, and another saying that until such time as the kingdoms were reunited, I would remain my father's heir and would succeed him in my own right, and on my accession to the throne of Eswy (Huvehla and Geneh willing), Dugald would take the title of Consort in Eswy and I of Consort in Dunmorra.

"That's how it's done in Talverdin," Dugald remarked, "but we won't tell your barons that just yet."

The scribes made copies of these documents, and we signed and sealed them all, for evidence, for archives, for hope for the future. They were not legal treaties, but they showed our intent and would, we hoped, be evidence against those in Eswy who said I was abducted and the marriage invalid, or those in Dunmorra who would believe that Dunmorra now ruled Eswy.

Amidst all the diplomacy, the historians and the clerks and the lawyers debating tradition and law, I wanted us both to remember that the marriage was more.

There is an old country song called "I Shall Go to My Love in the Moonlight." I could not fall asleep the night before my wedding. I sat up by the window, working by candlelight in the cool mountain air, and I composed a new tune for the song, arranging it for flute and lute. *The Rose Maiden—for Dugald*, I wrote across the top of the sheet.

I signed it with an *E* crowned with roses, rather than the spray of roses I had used when I gave my pieces to Lovell to play with his friends. Then I could sleep, for the few hours left of the night. In the morning, I rolled up the composition, tied it with a thin braid of my hair and had a page take it to the king.

I choked down a little bread and milk at breakfast, but that was all I could manage. The women dressed me in a gown of white and gold brocade, with a coronet of pearls, a gift from the Queen of Talverdin, no less, in my hair. When I saw myself in the mirror, as Baroness Oakhold and her two waiting-women put the final touches to my attire by tucking silver-pink rosebuds into my crown of braids, I found myself gazing at a stranger: an elegant, graceful, beautiful woman. I swear I looked over my shoulder for her.

Dugald wore white and gold as well and looked a king in every line. Even his brother, with skin snow-pale and dressed in the Nightwalker fashion, his long tunic embroidered all over with brilliant and impossible plants and beasts, and Baroness Oakhold, all in sky-blue, on his arm, did not outshine my husband.

"Rose-girl," Dugald said to me, when Maurey and Annot led us to our horses, the first part of the ceremony. That was all, but there was so much in the words.

We rode in procession, with both courts around us, to make offerings of grain and wine and butter at a simple little shrine, dedicated to all seven Great Powers, just inside the gates of the town. The people of Greyrock turned out to watch and threw flowers and sweet herbs beneath our horses' hooves. We circled through the town, so that everyone could see us and know their king truly was marrying (so Annot cynically said), and then we went back up the road to the castle. There, in a quiet green corner where two birch trees embraced an old gray altar, we burned a ring, braided from our hair, with sweet and bitter herbs and spoke the old, old promises to one another before Geneh, Great Power of birth and death. The magistrates of the town solemnly recorded the marriage in their book of records: Dugald, son of Burrage, heir of Hallow the Great, King of Dunmorra, wed Eleanor, daughter of Hiram, heir of Hallow the Great, Crown Princess of Eswy, with six witnesses signing their names to swear it was so.

There was a great feast in the castle and another for the folk of Greyrock Town. I had little appetite, and less after the scandalous baroness whispered in my ear, "Eat! You'll need your strength." Maurey pulled her away and whatever he whispered in *her* ear made her blush and glance up at him with a look that, well, I thought perhaps Dugald had looked at me that way, when I came down into the castle yard in my bridal finery to ride to the town, but I was sure a virtuous young lady was not supposed to notice or feel astonished and glad and humbled by it.

They escorted us to the king's bedchamber with torches and quite rude songs, which seemed to be a Dunmorran tradition that the Nightwalkers found very strange and a little embarrassing, though I noticed some of the younger Nightwalker knights joining cheerfully in the songs once they figured out the words. Then we were left alone, and with a sigh of relief Dugald shut the door on the anteroom where his bodyguard stayed.

He also checked the underside of the bed for cowbells— another peculiar Dunmorran tradition—and threw them clanging out the window when he found them.

"That was definitely Annot and the Moss'avver," he said. "No one else would dare. I should have insisted the physicians keep Korby in bed another week."

His lute was lying on the table. I walked over and looked. He had my new composition there. "Did you have time to play it through?" I asked.

"I made time," he said. Then he laughed. "I'll have to practice more, if I'm to play with you. The fingering's almost beyond my skill."

"Did you like it?" I was so nervous my voice shook.

"Beautiful," he said, and then he was behind me, setting aside the pearls, undoing the ribbons, pulling out the pins with which Annot and her women had dressed my hair. He combed the braids out with his fingers. I turned around to look up at him and found I was not nervous at all.

PART THREE

✣ CHAPTER FOURTEEN ✣
ELEANOR: RETURN TO RENSEY

After Queen Ancrena and her people returned to Talverdin, our main concern was Eswy. There was no point waiting to see what Sawfield would do next. By means of a warlock magical device Maurey had left with the Dunmorran ambassador in Rensey, Dugald had almost daily news from Eswy, and it was not good. Baron Sawfield's nephew Gillem called himself "Lord of the Regency Council"; my mother was besieged in Narmor Castle by an alliance of southern barons, supporters of Sawfield; and my father had not been seen since shortly after Lovell's death. Some rumors said he had died, but the ambassador's spies—I was not able to be shocked or angry that the ambassador had spies—reported he was confined to his apartments in Rensey Palace, though whether a prisoner, or truly mad with grief as Gillem claimed, the ambassador did not know. The Hallalandish ambassador was threatening to blockade the port unless the queen was granted safe passage out of the country, and in the south a minor war had broken out between two neighboring baronies, scuffling for possession of the royal tin mines. Sawfield, when he returned to the city some three weeks after whatever had happened in the Westwood— both the prince and the Moss'avver were a little vague on that when I asked—began trying to muster the baronial troops for war, to rescue the "abducted and defiled princess" from the hands of the evil Nightwalkers. We had to act quickly, and did. However, even the king could not ready an army overnight, and the Eswyn baronry was not so swift to respond to Sawfield's call as he had hoped. Perhaps they were afraid my husband was preparing armies of warlocks to oppose them. Perhaps—I prayed to the Powers that it was so—they felt a lingering loyalty to their imprisoned king. Korby, though, said that most likely they were unwilling to leave their own provinces undefended, as neighbor eyed neighbor in a land where law was crumbling.

The meat-fast of Melkinas, the summer month sacred to Mayn of the Swelling Udders as Mother of Beasts, was over, and Morronas was on us, hot and green and golden or misty with rain, when we finally marched towards the border. Only three months had passed since I fled my mother's scheming, but I felt I had lived a lifetime.

Rensey is cradled in the arms of two rivers, the joining of the Esta and the Dortha. The northern bank of the Esta is Dunmorran soil—a poor place to put your chief city, right on the border, but that small southeastern corner of Dunmorra had once been Eswyn, until we lost a war. Now two bridge-castles glared at one another, an arrow-shot apart.

Queen Consort of Dunmorra and Heir of Eswy, I rode to the border. I rode under the banners of Dunmorra and of Eswy, and dressmakers in Cragroyal, where we had spent a brief few days, had made me into a banner myself, a statement of all I claimed to be. The divided skirts of my riding gown were mourning-blue for Lovell, with as many red Eswyn roses as there had been time to embroider scattered over them. My bodice was the brighter Dunmorran royal blue, my sleeves Eswyn red and gold. Lord Romner had reclaimed his Sennanna and my horse was a dun Korlander mare, a wedding gift from the Oakhold stables, caparisoned in red and blue. Later on, artists painted the scene—Queen Eleanor crossing the Esta—but they always made me very beautiful, older than I was, and they left out the rain. I never wrote a song about it, but in all likelihood the Rose Maiden would have left out the rain too.

"Anaskto with me," I muttered under my breath, and with a glance at the men and women to either side of me, I started my horse out onto the echoing wooden bridge. It was time to discover how Eswy would greet its returning heir.

The garrison at the castle on the Eswyn side of the bridge over the Esta let us pass without challenge or welcome. We certainly had not taken them by surprise; the main body of our forces was encamped three miles from the border on Lancelin Hill, waiting to see what happened, and I doubt Sawfield had neglected to have spies and informers in Dunmorra watching—us?—them? Was I Dunmorran or Eswyn? Did I have to choose? Was I going to end up like Prince Maurey, who seemed to be neither wholly Talverdine nor wholly Dunmorran?

Dunmorran heralds proclaimed me as we rode through the open gates and into the city of Rensey: "Eleanor, Queen Consort of Dunmorra, Crown Princess of Eswy."

The city gates closed behind us. I took a deep breath. I had expected that. I looked at the man riding to my left. They would take him for some knight or young lord. The surcoat over his armor, the device on his shield and the trappings of his piebald Kordaler stallion showed a black tower on a gold ground, scattered with red roses. The Eswyn heralds would be puzzling over that, trying to place him, but the arms were new, my own, combining elements of the royal arms of Dunmorra and Eswy. Dugald winked at me.

No one had wanted him to cross into Eswy. He should wait with the army. Even I had thought it too dangerous. Korby—the Moss'avver, as I had learned I should properly call him—had shouted at him. Dunmorrans seemed inclined to speak their minds, and Fenlanders, I was discovering, were not in awe of any mere descendent of Good King Hallow. They claimed to have been in Eswiland even before the Nightwalkers, though I did not believe it.

Dugald had shouted right back, "Am I to sit chewing my nails with the army, waiting to hear she's been captured by that brute Sawfield? You expect me to let her go into a danger I hide from? To ride into a trap like that without me by her side?"

The rest of Dugald's barons and captains were just as much against the idea as Korby, though they had tried to make reasonable arguments without shouting. Even I had found the courage to argue that if Sawfield was so openly treasonous as to take me prisoner with the eyes of all Rensey on him, he would not scruple to seize Dugald too, and thus hold a knife to Dunmorra's throat.

Dugald said he was coming with me, and that was the end of it. I was discovering I had married a very stubborn man.

Secretly, I was very glad he was by my side. I had Captain Lord Anders, who commanded Dugald's bodyguard, and that bodyguard of knights and men-at-arms, all in full armor. I had the Moss'avver, whom everyone seemed to regard as a champion to be respected and feared. As outriders I had a dozen of Korby's Fenlanders in light armor, armed with glaives—an edged blade on a long pole, a favorite Fen weapon—mounted on stocky black ponies. I had Baroness Oakhold and two of her women, Lady Ursula and Margo, who, I had been astonished to learn, had been born a cowherd's daughter, though she could read and write and now served Annot as a waiting-woman. They were decently dressed in full-skirted riding gowns, though their high-necked, velvet-covered jackets were lined with steel plates and all three were armed. Annot claimed most men would not look beyond the skirts to notice their swords, and if they did, they would dismiss the weapons as pretty fancies, toys for girls playing games. She called herself and her women my bodyguard of last resort. If enemies reached us through all the other guards we had…well, they would at least be surprised before we died.

To make us look less warlike, it was Margo and Lady Ursula who carried the banners of Dunmorra and of Eswy behind me, the silver-rayed black tower on blue and the red rose on gold keeping pace with one another.

Somewhere, invisible in the halfworld, I had the Warden of Greyrock and some of his Nightwalker retinue, which was in truth the only reason the king's captains had allowed him to accompany me.

But still, it was Dugald's presence that made me feel a queen. He believed I could do this. He believed I could win back my country and save us from war. He gambled his freedom, maybe his life, on his faith in me.

That terrified me, but it lifted me up too, as though I flew on powerful wings: a falcon, an eagle. I did not need to depend on the Rose Maiden, though she would always be a part of me. I was Eleanor of Eswy and Dunmorra, and she was much, much stronger.

A fine drizzle was falling and the streets were nearly empty. There were knots of city-watch at the main intersections. Sawfield had imposed a curfew on the city.

Why? I asked myself.

Because the populace was dangerous. But to whom? Would a ravening mob tear me limb from limb, screaming about the invasion of Dunmorran kale-eaters and evil Nightwalkers? Or did he fear the folk of Rensey would rise for the king, if only someone would lead them?

"There are people watching from their windows," Baroness Oakhold murmured.

I nodded and glanced over at Korby. He looked very far away; he always seemed to whenever there were crowds of people around.

He looked dangerous. I thought that if I were a citizen of Rensey, I might have been lurking indoors, peeking out at him in fear too. He was riding Boots, because he said Boots was better in crowds, but in black plate armor on the big black stallion, with his visor raised on his scarred face and that remote cold look in his eye, he did not look like a peaceful queen's escort. It was he who drew the eyes of the nervous guardsmen on the corner, not Dugald, not Captain Lord Anders, not the other two barons who attended me.

"The people of Eswy are not our enemies," I said aloud. I needed to remind myself.

I reined in Veery, my mare, and stood in the stirrups, looking up at the houses on either side. This was Wool Street, lined with the dwellings and warehouses of prosperous merchants. They traded with Dunmorra, with Hallaland and Rona and Hallsia, with distant Gehtaland and Rossmark; they lived by sifting the truth of rumor and the whisperings of courts.

"What news of the king?" I shouted at the windows. "Does Baron Sawfield still hold him prisoner?"

Even the watchmen on the corner looked interested, though no one called down an answer. If the ambassador's information was correct, I knew the answer anyway. I merely wanted to make certain the onlookers knew it.

"I am Eleanor of Eswy, Queen Consort of Dunmorra. I am my father's only heir, by right of my blood, by right of his choice, by right of declaration in the Council of Barons. I do not come in conquest; my lord husband does not come to claim the Eswyn crown. I come to save Eswy from the traitor Sawfield, who murdered my beloved brother, murdered wise Prince Lovell."

I was giving them poetry, phrases that could be from a song. I was using Lovell to win their sympathy and I hated myself for it, but at the same time it was true: he was beloved, he was wise, or he might have been had he lived to grow into the promise of his youth. Whoever had killed him—and I still did not know if it was Sawfield—had stolen that from him and from all of Eswy.

"Sawfield thought he could marry me by force and take the crown for himself. I come to save Eswy from Sawfield, who treacherously holds my father captive in Rensey Palace, if he has not already foully slain him. Good people, people of Rensey, come with me to demand that the Council of Barons bring me my father, your king. In the name of Huvehla, the Weaver of Fate, in the name of Great Phaydos, help me to save Eswy from this poison of treason that rots the heart of our land. Help me to free my father, Geneh granting he still lives, and restore him to his rightful place. Follow me, I beseech you."

The Rose Maiden knew how to stir hearts. I watched faces move behind windows.

Korby spoke to one of his Moss'avver retainers in some language that sounded like flowing water, one moment sharp and bright, the next shushing and coughing. Fen speech bore no relation to any civilized tongue and there was no chance any onlooker would understand. The woman wheeled her black pony and trotted away down a side-street.

"Where is she going?" Dugald asked quietly.

"The ambassador's house," said the Moss'avver. "Maurey might have left a message. Right?" he asked the empty air, but of course there was no answer. If the prince or any of the Nightwalkers were with us in the halfworld, we would not know.

"How do we know you're the real princess?" a watchman demanded from the corner. They made no move to follow the Fenlander. Perhaps that was a good omen.

"Wait here," I told Captain Lord Anders. I touched my heels to Veery and rode forward slowly towards the men. Both Korby and Dugald moved as if they would follow me, and I waved them back. Annot, Lady Ursula and Margo came after me, though, and clustered close. The unarmed heralds spread out one to either side.

"That's a reasonable question," I told the man who had spoken, though I kept my voice raised and glanced up at the windows again. There were people in doorways now and sifting out into the street. "You all know I was raised in my mother's household and came far too rarely to court. But you all know my father was never a king to hide himself from his people, until now, and I do not believe he remains hidden in the palace by his own will. But you all remember his face. You all know my brother Lovell, Geneh keep him, went out among the people of the city. Many of you will have seen him. Look at me. Do you doubt I am my father's daughter, my brother's sister?"

I had never before been glad of my too-narrow face and the wash-faded blue of my eyes, though Dugald, bless his kindness, said I was beautiful.

I did not give the guardsmen time to begin to worry about what might happen. "I am Eleanor of Eswy," I said. "Follow me. Sawfield's treason is an outrage to Holy Anaskto, whose hand lies over lawful kings. Help me to overturn his treachery, in the name of the Seven Great Powers."

And I rode on, without looking back. My company trotted to catch up, sweeping around me.

"Your Grace, *don't* do that again," Captain Lord Anders implored. "We can't protect you if you separate yourself from us."

But Dugald murmured, "Nicely done, Rose-girl."

"They're following," Korby said.

"The guards?" I did not want to be seen peering around, as if I doubted. I had lost what little breakfast I had been able to eat before we set out and my stomach was churning again. This was worse than playing in front of a crowd for the first time.

"Half the street," Anders answered. "And they're running off into the city too, excited. They'll bring others. We shouldn't let ourselves get encircled by a mob, Your Grace, even if they are on Her Grace the queen's side."

"There's not much we can do to prevent it," Dugald said. "Try not to provoke them to violence, on either side."

"Powers be with us," muttered Captain Lord Anders.

Anaskto was with me. The Powers knew the justice of my cause. Part of me believed that. The Rose Maiden knew it was easy to give people a story they could care about, but a ballad was not the real world, and Sawfield was not going to fall to his knees and confess his crimes.

A vast crowd followed us by the time we reached Rensey Palace, on the southern edge of the city overlooking the joining of the two rivers. They were not a mob, not yet. My name rose and fell on a tide of voices.

The gates of the palace were closed. The heralds cried my name and titles and demanded entrance.

"They're fighting in the guard tower," Korby said. I do not know how he knew, but the fight was over almost as soon as it began. Men-at-arms in royal livery, red and gold, opened the gates to us, and as we rode in I glimpsed a man in Sawfield's yellow and black lying still in a doorway.

The crowd pressed in on the heels of the Fenlander rearguard. Citizens swarmed into the guard tower, climbed to the parapet of the wall. These gates would not be closed behind us.

Banners hung from the battlements of the hall where the barons' council traditionally met; the Redhall, it was called, from the color of its stone. They showed which barons were in attendance at court. I did not know enough of my own land to read them all, or to know which were friend or foe, or could be persuaded to my side. The heralds named off the baronies, and it was Dugald who muttered, "He'll be for Hiram, he's Sawfield's ally, he's for anyone who opposes the queen and Hallaland…"

The royal banner was flying, but of course, it would be. Baron Sawfield claimed my father was keeping to his apartments in Rensey Palace, overcome with grief at Lovell's death.

Most of the palace was a new building, built by my grandfather in a time of peace. He had run the crown of Eswy heavily into debt to build this place; that was why he had married my father to the princess of wealthy Hallaland. It swept wide, graceful wings to either side of the old Redhall, and there were windows even at ground level, most of them glazed. It was not a building that could be easily defended, but since we had left the Dunmorran army behind, it did not have to be.

We left the horses standing in the paved courtyard, with some of the men-at-arms to guard them, and entered Redhall on foot. Any guards posted there had disappeared. Were they waiting to see who won? I had never been to the council hall and did not know the way, but a bowing Eswyn herald appeared to fling open wide doors and say, "Welcome, Your Grace."

I tried to fix his face in memory. He seemed genuinely pleased to see me. There was a stir in the crowd as we crossed the threshold, a man on horseback forcing his way through. I looked back. Not a man—the Fenlander woman Korby had sent to the ambassador. She swung from her pony and squirmed after us, elbowing any who got in her way.

"M'lord," she panted, and then gabbled some long message of which I understood not a word. Korby grinned his lopsided grin, though, and gave her a slap on the shoulder as though she really were just one of his men.

"Your father's safe, Your Grace," Korby said, for my ears and Dugald's alone. "He's locked in an apartment on the upper floor at the end of the east wing, guarded by Sawfield's men.

Maurey's lads went in off the roof last night. They were going to stay with him, hidden, just in case of trouble. Better if you're the one to free him, though."

I nodded my understanding. Maurey's Nightwalkers would rescue my father if Sawfield decided to make sure he fell down the stairs before I arrived, but otherwise they would merely wait, guarding him secretly. If the king appeared surrounded by Nightwalkers and accused Sawfield of treachery, the baron would cry that the king had been imprisoned and bespelled by the warlocks. It should be my own people who exposed Sawfield's treason and rescued my father.

The chamber we entered was long, with ranks of benches facing one another across a central aisle. Two curving staircases led to a gallery over the door, which was where my great-grandfather had stationed archers when he summoned his barons. On one occasion he had ordered them to shoot. By the time I remembered that story, we had already emerged from beneath the overhang, but even as Korby looked up and put himself between me and any assassin there, a handful of the city-watch and a crowd of the citizens were pouring up the stairs. A few shouts and some cheering floated down.

"Carry on, Highness!" a man called, leaning over the parapet.

I raised a hand to acknowledge him. I found out later there had been two crossbowmen stationed in the gallery, with orders to shoot Dugald if he accompanied me, but they had thrown down their weapons and declared for me as the tide flowed up the stairs.

The council chamber was by no means full. More than half the barons had stayed away from Rensey. Those present had their own knights and clerks about them, but no one was sitting on the benches in debate. They stood in small clusters, nearly all armed and many in full or half-armor, as if they expected a battlefield.

Of course, they were afraid of Nightwalkers stepping from the shadows to murder them.

I had to remember they were not a unified army but a number of gangs, and each gang would decide for itself which side to join, like brawlers outside a seafront tavern.

Baron Sawfield stood on the top of the three steps that led to my father's throne. He gripped the arm of the great chair of state, with its carved and gilded roses, as though it were already his.

"Eleanor, my dear," he said, "I'm so glad to see you safe. We heard you were in the hands of the Dunmorran's tame warlock. Thank the Powers you've escaped." His eyes searched the company around me and did not linger on Dugald.

Sawfield was a thickset man, handsome in a dull sort of way, like a pampered tomcat. I remembered seeing him at court. He had ignored me, in those days, or spoken to me as though I were a simpleton. Now he had chosen to meet me dressed in royal scarlet hose and boots and gilded half-armor; it made his face look flushed. At least he was not wearing the Eswyn rose—yet.

"Why should I need to escape, lord baron?" I asked. "My brother died, most foully murdered, and I fled to the safety of my betrothed husband's kingdom. I have returned, with my husband's blessing and aid, to demand you release my father."

"You have been tricked by Dunmorran lies, dear child. King Hiram, Geneh preserve him, is safe, though broken in health and mind by your brother's tragic death and your abduction."

I took a deep breath. "No, my lord," I said, "I will not accept that answer. I know my father is fully in command of his wits. I know you have him imprisoned in the palace." I looked over the barons and nobles assembled in the chamber, pulled together what I remembered Lovell saying of them and Dugald's tallying of them as we saw the banners.

"My lord Nestoring, my lord Tarus, Baron Durford." I named a man I knew my father had trusted, a friend of Lovell's, and a man all admired for his rigid honor. "Do me the grace of taking some of your men as witnesses and accompanying Sir Iohn Springhill. Sir Iohn, take six men and release my father. Baron Sawfield has him imprisoned in an apartment on the upper floor of the east wing."

Sir Iohn, the lieutenant of Dugald's bodyguard, slid his eyes to his king. Dugald gave the faintest of nods. Of course he had to check before leaving the king's presence. I hoped Baron Sawfield had not noticed that little exchange, though.

"Lord Gillem!" I raised my voice, as Sir Iohn, Lord Nestoring and the others I had named moved slowly through the crowd to reach the main doors. "Where are *you* going?"

I had been watching for some such sneaking. A young man at the back of the cluster of Sawfield's knights had slipped towards a door in the paneled wall. Gillem was the son of Sawfield's mistress, Lovell had said, though the baron had brought him to court as his nephew. He had been his so-called uncle's right hand in all his treason: my father's jailer, "Lord of the Regency Council."

With all those eyes on him, Lord Gillem, and the two knights accompanying him, hesitated. The Moss'avver made some abrupt movement.

"*There's* the prince's killer for you," he muttered to the king.

"Who?" Dugald demanded.

"That—Gillem, Her Grace called him? Tall skinny fellow sneaking out the back with the Sawfield knights."

"Are you certain?" Dugald asked.

"How do you know?" I demanded.

Dugald gave me a brief glance and shook his head. He wanted me to let it go for now. Back in the Westwood, Maurey had made some joke about Korby being a witch, but he could not seriously have expected me to believe it. Everyone said things like that about barbarians, and it did not seem fair to Korby to let him be blamed that way, to hide the fact they—we—had spies even in Rensey Palace.

"Same feel ta 'im," I thought Korby might have said, but his accent was suddenly so thick I could not be sure. "Murder in his mind now, f'certain."

Lord Gillem bolted for the door. Suddenly it did not matter to me how Korby knew.

"Stop him!" I screamed. "He murdered my brother! Don't let him reach the king!"

An Eswyn man-at-arms, in the royal livery, roared wordlessly and flung himself at Gillem as the young lord wrenched at the door. They both struck the floor with a clash and thud and struggled up, grappling with one another, too close to draw swords. A knife flashed and the soldier staggered, but another man was there, and another, lords and lords' men, and they wrestled Gillem's weapons from him and held him pinioned. Sawfield's retainers had not moved to help him.

"Don't listen to the lying chit!" Gillem cried. "She's nothing but a Dunmorran trollop; she's sold you all to the north! She's mad as her brother, mad as her father—Anaskto has cursed them. She's brought the warlocks down on you. Holy Anaskto has turned his face from the whole family—the crown must pass to a new line—"

"You were seen." Dugald interrupted Gillem's shrill rant. "You hid yourself in shadow, disguised in the gown of a university master."

"No."

"At the top of a flight of stairs. You hid a cudgel in your sleeve."

Korby watched Gillem as a cat watches a mouse. The young lord flushed angry red. "What lies!"

"You struck the prince," said my husband remorselessly, his voice growing soft, "from behind, like a coward."

Gillem's face was white now, not white like a Nightwalker's, but like an ill man's: gray, with a sheen of sweat. "You're mad, whoever you are."

"Do not lie!" Dugald thundered. "You were seen! The prince fell. You watched him fall, and then you walked away, as if you'd dispatched a fowl for the table, and left him lying."

"And where was this supposed watcher?" Gillem asked. He tried to make it a sneer, but his voice shook. I could almost see the tide of fear rising in him. But I hoped Dugald would answer his question. I too wanted to know what spy had seen my brother murdered and done nothing to prevent it.

"One of Dunmorra's tame warlocks, was it, lurking in the darkness? If murder was done, do we need to look further than that?"

"Swear it," said the Moss'avver. "Swear by the Seven Great Powers and the shade of Prince Lovell that you were not the man who killed him."

I would have protested—a man who would cold-bloodedly murder his prince would certainly perjure himself and swear a false oath to save his life—but again, Dugald shook his head, ever so slightly. Something, certainly, was making Gillem very afraid, as though for the first time in his life he felt the eyes of Fescor and Geneh on him in judgement. He shook his head and licked his lips.

"Speak up, nephew, and deny this fool knight's lie," said Sawfield.

"I…I did not…I…Let me go!" Gillem screamed, struggling to pull away from the men who held him. "It had to be done! Lovell corrupted us with foreign ideas, he and his base-born student friends. It was he, he sold the princess to the Dunmorrans; he had all Eswy in his hand and he counted it nothing. He, a prince! He debased Hallow's blood in every act. Fawning on the kale-eaters and pandering his sister to them! Barbarian orgies in the taverns with Gehtalanders and Rossians, even with their mannish women!"

"Ah, that'd be old Earl Jans' poetry evenings, no doubt," someone murmured, but nobody laughed.

"Setting up some peasant wanton as a lady minstrel and flaunting her works at court—at this very court—as though such a one could ever be blessed by Ayas. How long before he'd have brought her out and you'd have all been forced to bow and scrape to her, a half-witted little slavey aping the arts the Powers intended to enrich the lives of those of noble birth? How long before we were all bending the knee to some bastard-born peasant princeling? Lovell had his dotard father wrapped around his little finger; he'd have got any son of this Rose Harlot of his declared his heir, you know he would have, and we'd have found ourselves ruled by a peasant in another generation, while the true line of Hallow's blood was forgotten."

"Now that's the pot calling the kettle black," murmured the same Eswyn knight who had commented before.

I found myself shaking with fury. "*I* am the Rose Maiden," I hissed. "Fescor damn you, how dare you defame my brother's very memory so! Isn't it enough you robbed him of his life?"

"Take him to the prince's tomb and have him swear his oath by Lovell's shade there!" a woman called from the gallery.

"Doesn't want to, does he?"

"Can't say the words. The Powers freeze his tongue."

"Choke on your oath, murderer!"

Lord Gillem yelled and wrenched himself free. He ran only a few strides before the royal men-at-arms seized him once more.

"Kill him!" roared a voice from the back of the crowd. "Kill the murderer! Kill the traitor!"

Other voices took up the call. The sound rose into a snarling storm, a mindless churning flood of bloodlust. Those at the back were starting to press forward; in the gallery they were crowding towards the stairs, and those at the bottom of the stairs were fighting to get away into the lower crowd before they were crushed. Only in the front rows were they more cautious, facing our armed company and all the barons' retainers. But the ones at the back, uncaring, not at the sword's edge themselves, pushed them on.

In a moment the Redhall was going to be a battleground, and once they started killing, would they stop with Sawfield's people? Dunmorrans had been an enemy too often.

Captain Anders snapped an order, and a wall of Dunmorran knights closed up around Dugald and me.

✼ CHAPTER FIFTEEN ✼
ELEANOR: DEATH AT THE BARONS' COUNCIL

"Get that mob settled!" Korby snarled at me. "They're yours, Your Grace. Quiet them or there'll be a massacre. Once they start, they'll be dogs among the sheep, and no caring who they tear apart."

He was right. I had come to take back my father's kingdom, not to slaughter his subjects, or to be trampled by them.

"Move back!" I ordered Dugald's knights. "Give me room." They did so, reluctantly.

I raised both hands and prayed no one saw how they shook. "Good people, peace!" I shouted, and to my astonishment the rising rumble of voices stilled. So did the advance of the crowd. People stood on tiptoe, straining to see, to listen. "My brother valued justice above all else; we will have *justice* for him, not bloody barbarian vengeance. We are Eswyn. We keep the traditions of ancient Rona, where law ensured justice for all. If Gillem is denied a fair trial, how can any of you trust to have one, should you be accused of a crime? Law applies to the strong as well as the weak, to the noble as well as the commons, and when it does not, all suffer and Geneh turns her head away in shame. We have heard Gillem's confession, but once my father is restored there will be a trial. A *trial*, where we will learn the truth. So peace, now. Let us honor Lovell's memory by keeping the peace in his name. Let us show our Dunmorran friends— my dear husband's people—that we are a nation who love justice and reason, not barbarians who answer murder with murder."

Dugald raised an eyebrow. I suppose that I had rather suggested that Dunmorrans might be more like barbarians than we were, but that was what most Eswyns thought anyway, and it was an Eswyn mob that I had to somehow inspire, or shame, into calm. He shrugged as the restless movement reversed, people fighting their way back to the best vantage points in the gallery and on the stairs.

The Moss'avver sighed. "Good," he told me. He looked to me as though he was having another of those bad headaches to which he was prone. He really needed to consult a decent physician. Master Findley would probably recommend poppy wine and bleeding, but I could imagine Korby's response to that: It would not be him bleeding.

I had quieted the mob just in time. The Dunmorran knights and Eswyn lords I had sent to find my father returned. He walked among them—oh, he looked so old. He had always been old to my childish eyes, not a young man even when he married my mother, and weary from trying to rein in the barons, but it seemed to me there was far more white in his hair than there had been in the spring, and his face was lined and pallid, with a hectic flush of red on his cheekbones. For a moment I felt a pang of fear that Sawfield had been right and the king was sinking into his dotage, but his gaze, as he looked around the chamber, was alert and steady. He was ill, not feeble-minded.

"Eleanor!" he cried, seeing me. "They said you had come. And Queen of Dunmorra—the Powers be thanked."

"Sir," I said, and curtseyed. There was such pride in his voice.

But our reunion was interrupted by a shriek.

"Eleanor! Eleanor, tell them to let me go!"

A brief struggle erupted behind the king. Katerina. I signalled the Dunmorran knights to bring her forward.

She was modestly, though elegantly, dressed in a gown of mourning blue. For Lovell? I wondered. It seemed an excessive display, if so. He was not *her* brother. Was she declaring herself to be no longer my mother's agent, by dressing in a manner a Penitent should disdain?

"We found this girl too, in the antechamber of the king's apartment with the guards," one of Dugald's knights explained. "With this." He held out a stone mortar, a quarter filled with some yellowish paste, with lumps of white in it. It did not look to me like anything one would grind up for use in the kitchen.

Another held up a small casket, open to reveal an array of stoppered jars—definitely not spices. Oh, Katerina, I thought, and my heart felt full of lead. Despite everything, she was still dear, for all the secrets we had shared, for all the friendship she had given me when I was so alone. Like a sister, I could not hate her. She, at least, had not betrayed me for any selfish gain. She had no greed for crowns and power. Foolish though it was, she truly feared the Nightwalkers in Dunmorra; she only did what she thought was best for me, though of course she had no right to decide that.

"We don't know what she was doing. Brewing up some alchemical poison, most likely."

"For his protection!" Katerina screamed, again struggling against the two soldiers who gripped her arms. "The warlocks were coming for the king. I knew they would send warlocks for him, I had to make protection, and now it's too late, too late..." She dissolved into tears.

"Lady Katerina," I said, "give me your word, by Holy Huvehla and all the Seven Powers together, that this was no poison and that you intended no harm to the king."

Katerina sagged to her knees, and the knights let her down, still gripping her shoulders.

"Your Highness—"

"Your Grace," the Moss'avver corrected coldly. He had never liked Katerina.

"Your Grace, I swear by Huvehla and Phaydos and Mayn and all the Powers, I never intended harm to the king. All I did, I did for love of you, to preserve you and your honor and safety."

"What alchemy were you preparing in the king's chamber?"

"Where did you learn alchemy?" demanded the Moss'avver. He might have been able to scare Gillem into a confession, but Katerina ignored his cold glower.

"A…a recipe…," she stuttered, answering me. "Something I found in an old book."

"Philosopher's fire," said Dugald, as though he spoke of something obscene.

"No!" The look Katerina gave him was almost one of disdain. "It's a…a compound that repels them, like, like woodruff and moths. I thought the king was in danger from warlocks. I meant to protect him."

"Katerina, any warlocks here are my allies."

"Yes, Your Grace. I beg your pardon. I…I understand that now."

"And you shouldn't experiment with alchemical compounds when you have no education in alchemy. You could have poisoned yourself or even the king and everyone in the room, if that mess caught fire!"

"I'm sorry, Your Grace, so sorry. Can you…how can you ever forgive me?" She was weeping, her face blotched and red. Not even Katerina was pretty when she cried. "Oh, Eleanor, I loved you like a sister. I only wanted to do what was best. I'm so sorry, so sorry…"

I would have run to her then, but the Rose Maiden knew that this was not the time. The Queen of Dunmorra, the Crown

Princess of Eswy, could not be seen by her barons blubbering with her friend like a pair of little girls who had quarrelled and made up.

"We'll talk of this later, Katerina, my dear," I said. "For now, do I have your word you will have no more to do with Sawfield and his plots? And your promise you won't dabble in alchemy again?"

"Yes, Your Grace, I swear it. I do. Only don't despise me. Don't send me away from you. My father will never take me back, not after this. I can't go home to Hallaland. Say you forgive me, I beg you."

"Of course I do," I said.

What else could I have done? I could not be hard and heartless, like my mother, or take some cruel revenge on her. If I cast Katerina off, where could she go? I could not condemn her to imprisonment or death as a traitor, not Katerina, who had danced in the Old Keep and kept the secret of my music. I could not even turn her adrift to fend for herself. A young woman alone in a foreign land has no hope.

"But we'll speak of these things later," I said. "There are more important matters to deal with. Baron Sawfield—"

I should have stepped aside then, and let my father take the lead, but I am ashamed to say it did not even occur to me. Nor did it occur to me that I should have ordered Sawfield arrested like his nephew, before I began accusing him of crimes for which he would have to pay with his head—if they were proven.

"Baron, I accuse you of treason, here before the Council of Barons. You may have helped to plan my brother's murder; we do not know that yet. You certainly took full advantage of it. You attempted to seize my person, intending marriage whether I would or no. You attacked me and those who tried to protect me in the Westwood. You have kept the king, your liege lord, imprisoned in his own palace. What do you say to this?"

"I only wanted what was best for Eswy, Your Highness," Sawfield said. Katerina had made almost the same argument, but I felt no urge to forgive him. "I would have made you queen of a strong land, a land that could not be threatened by foreigners and the unclean elements of the north."

"The Powers willing, I will be queen someday, may Huvehla long preserve my father—queen of a proud and honorable land, lord baron," I said, "a land where justice does not mean death for the weak and the powerless at the whim of the mighty…" All there knew his reputation for harsh and arbitrary punishments of the peasants unfortunate enough to live in his barony. "And no one here is threatening Eswy but you."

"The Powers will judge me, Highness," he said. He drew his sword. Everyone around me tensed. Stiffly, Baron Sawfield lowered himself to his knees and held out the naked blade across his hands. "I surrender my sword to you, Eleanor, as I would have surrendered my heart and hand and a free land."

"Don't," the Moss'avver said, but I had already taken the few steps towards the baron, some coolly gracious answer on my lips. I wanted this over; I would accept Sawfield's surrender and have him taken out of my sight. Dugald reached out after me, but by then it was too late.

Sawfield's sword fell with a clatter as he seized me, bouncing to his feet and dragging me against him. I felt a pressure between my shoulder blades and froze before I could even start to struggle and scream. A gasp and a murmur of horror ran around the chamber and the crowded gallery.

"Eleanor!" my father cried.

"Release her. Drop the knife," Dugald said, his voice low with fury. "You won't escape."

"I think not. You will stand aside, sir knight, and allow us to pass. Eleanor will be my safe-conduct to my own lands in the south, and you may tell your master to come fetch her if he dares, that all may see the treachery of the Dunmorrans, who invade us to ravage our land and carry off our queen."

"She is not queen yet," my father said, his breath still uneven. "She will never be your queen, Sawfield. All here have witnessed your treachery. Let her go. You will have no allies, no friends. Abduct and dishonor my daughter and I will see you hanged like the base criminal you are, and welcome Dugald of Dunmorra across the Esta to tie the knot about your throat."

I had had no idea my father could spin words so skillfully. Even then, I felt a burst of pride in him.

"Dishonor? What dishonor is there in marriage to a nobleman of pure human blood, untainted by association with warlocks? I'm a descendant of Blessed Hallow, just as you are. I'm your own cousin's son. If we followed Ronish law and barred female inheritance of title and property, as Hallow's will laid out, I would be your heir."

"That will was proven a forgery," Dugald pointed out, "an attempt by Hallow's nephew to displace the king's granddaughter. That man died condemned by the Powers for his treason against the rightful queen."

It was all ancient history, part of the two generations of wars that had led to the creation of Eswy and Dunmorra out of Good King Hallow's kingdom of Eswiland, and it did not distract Sawfield into an empty argument, though that was probably what Dugald had hoped to do.

The baron released his grasp on me, but only for a moment. He jerked me around, seizing me again as I tried to throw myself away. Now my back was against his chest and he had one arm across my throat. Squinting down over it I could see the small knife he had pressed beneath my breast. I could feel his heaving chest. He was more afraid than his steady voice showed.

"Walk, my queen," he sneered. "We will take horse and ride for the south, and if the lords of the council wish to prove themselves true Eswyns, uncontaminated by the spells of the Dunmorran warlocks that corrupted your brother's mind, they will deal with these kale-eaters here and now and leave none to take word back to the coward abductor who so dishonored you. A forced marriage such as yours to the Dunmorran is no marriage before the Powers, and all here are witness you are free to wed me. Lady Katerina, if you would lead the way? Now walk, my dear. Stand aside, you!"

Dugald's knights shuffled a few paces aside. Behind them, the citizens of Rensey parted, muttering and scowling, leaving Sawfield a clear path to the door.

My eyes were on Dugald. I was hardly aware of anyone else: my father, looking old and sick and barely able to stand, leaning on Baroness Oakhold's arm. The Moss'avver like some dark and menacing creature of legend, not even human, a thunderstorm in armor. Captain Anders, furious and frustrated. I saw them, but they were dim and unimportant. The one who mattered was Dugald, standing tense and still, like a hound poised, scenting prey, ready to leap forward at a word. The knife dug into the quilted velvet of my bodice, and Sawfield's arm tightened around my neck as he forced me to step ahead with him. He probably could not feel how his vambrace pressed my rigid high collar cruelly into my throat.

Three steps. Four. At nine I would be within arm's reach of Dugald and he would seize me away, thrust me behind him as Sawfield was overwhelmed by Anders and the Moss'avver. Our two minds were working as one. Five. We even smiled, grim and knowing, joined by our eyes as if our hands already met and gripped. I felt oddly calm, almost floating, watching it all.

"Sawfield!" my father cried, and he snatched the sword from Annot's hand and rushed at the baron. Katerina looked back and, of course, screamed. Sawfield tried to twist us away, tripped, our feet entangled, and in saving himself from falling he punched me below the breast with the hand clenched on the hilt of the little blade. Cloth tore and something snapped. I shrieked in anger, seeing my father stumbling to the floor, knocked aside by one of Sawfield's men, but Katerina screamed louder.

"You've killed her! He's killed the princess! Sawfield has murdered the princess!"

"No!" Sawfield took a step away from her, dragging me stumbling with him. "No!" The muttering that had never completely died among the crowd fell into horrified silence. Had he killed me? I felt nothing. Perhaps that was what it was like to take a mortal wound.

Perhaps it was, but how was I to know? Killed me, nonsense.

Korby and Dugald were already leaping forward. I went limp, and Sawfield, still crying, "No! No!" dropped me to the floor, as though he could somehow rid himself of any connection with my poor bleeding corpse. He held a bloody hand and broken knife before his face as if he could not believe they were his. Then he began to bend, to reach for me again.

Maurey stepped out of the halfworld, a watery red light flaring around his arm, and struck Sawfield, open-palmed, in the chest. The man flew away from me, losing the knife. He fell and rolled and struggled to his feet coughing and gasping, but he had Annot's sword, dropped by my father, in his hand and he shrieked at his king, "What heir do you have now but me, you old fool?" as he raised the blade.

"Yes," said Dugald to Korby.

The Moss'avver took one more stride and with a two-handed blow of his greatsword—I thought what followed was poetry, a description for ballads, not something humans did to one another. I had never seen a battlefield. I never wanted to.

He clove Sawfield's skull to the jaw.

I shut my eyes. I did not need them open to know it was

Dugald who flung himself down on his knees and wrapped arms and armored body around me, sheltering me, his face buried in my hair. Then fingers were gently searching me, feeling the small sticky patch of blood below my breasts.

"His knife broke," I said and was surprised at how my voice shook. "He cut his own hand."

"I'll make Annot's dressmaker a lady," my husband said.

"And her armorer husband."

"He'd better be a knight. He wouldn't want to be a lady." But that was a silliness whispered into my hair, and only the two of us heard and giggled, drunk with life. Dugald helped me to my feet, and we stood before the eyes of the chamber and the gallery.

"Eleanor," my father whispered, sitting sprawled on the floor, arms and legs splayed around him.

"Armor," I said, tapping my chest. "A velvet brigandine." I would have gone to help him up, but Maurey was there before me. He offered the king his hand and my father, after only a moment's hesitation, took it. Once he was on his feet he remained leaning on Maurey's arm, his breath still wheezing. He shot sideways glances at the Nightwalker prince, but they were as much wonder as fear.

More muttering. Maurey was trapped with us in the rain-gray daylight of the council chamber. Korby, blood and I do not want to know what dripping from his blade, loomed suddenly at his friend's shoulder, and though no one had moved towards the Nightwalker who supported the king, there was a rustle of movement backwards.

"Father," I said, and curtseyed as a dutiful daughter should. I realized he had no idea who the man was who had held me so tightly. "My husband, Dugald of Dunmorra. My lord, my father, Hiram of Eswy."

They both bowed shallowly, as kings did.

"Prince Maurey of Talverdin, Warden of Greyrock Castle. The Moss'avver. Baroness Oakhold."

I introduced the other Dunmorran barons who had accompanied us, though that was properly the job of the heralds.

"I welcome you, with all my heart," my father said, and he let go of Maurey, cautiously, as though afraid he might fall, and came to clasp Dugald's hands. "Welcome, to you and your people—and to your kinsman, Prince Maurey." He said this all loudly, for the benefit of the great chamber, which was silent, not a whisper, as distant onlookers strained to hear. My father kissed my forehead and then gave up on formality and hugged me, hugged me hard as he had never done, in all our careful meetings at court.

I remembered how Maurey and Dugald had embraced, when the prince and Romner had finally reached us at Greyrock, with Korby fevered and gray in the wagon Dugald had sent. I had nearly wept, not jealous, but longing for the kind of love the brothers so obviously shared, feeling Lovell's loss fresh and raw. I held my father close as though I would never let him go, but finally I did, to take Dugald's arm again.

Someone at the back of the crowd began to cheer. I did not think Lovell's shade walked, but still, I felt him there with me. And I knew how the lament I would write for him should end, with that great rising tide of triumph and joy swelling and then dying into a quiet single voice, the bass flute alone, not mourning but soft and remembering and full of peace.

My father looked around and crossed to the nearest bench, onto which he climbed. He raised his hands, and the crowd fell silent.

"My daughter is well," he said. "She came prepared to meet with a traitor, with Anaskto's hand protecting her, and Sawfield's knife broke in his hand. He is justly slain for his treachery and

his treason against us. I call on you all to witness that it is by
my will she has married the noble King of Dunmorra, who has
risked his life to come here in support of her, not to seize Eswy
in her name, but to save me from the traitor Sawfield, for love
of her. I call on you all to witness that King Dugald's most
honorable Nightwalker allies have come not as our enemies, not
as assassins in the night, but to protect my daughter and to free
me from an ignoble captivity."

People murmured. I wondered where the other Nightwalkers
were. Perhaps all about us. They did not show themselves. They
did not trust us Eswyns so far. I cannot say I blamed them.

"I want," said my father, "a renewed oath of fealty from every
Eswyn baron in this chamber, and every knight and soldier and
servant of the royal household present—an oath to myself, and
to my daughter, the queen of Dunmorra, as my heir."

His eye sought and found an Eswyn herald. "Announce it."

"Shall we clear the chamber of the mob, Your Grace?" a
man-at-arms in the royal colors of Eswy asked. "They're all over
here and outside, all the way to the gate…"

"Oh no," said my father. "They came in support of Her
Grace Eleanor. They will remain to witness."

The flood of whispering that had started again swelled into
another cheer.

✣ CHAPTER SIXTEEN ✣
KORBY: HUNTING THE YEHILLON

There were three of us sitting at the table in the library overlooking the embassy rose garden, plus my cousin's hairy dog, who smelled, having earlier decided to cool himself off in the ornamental fishpond. The garden backed against the city wall, and beyond it, the Esta rolled, murky and brackish. Most of us would be over the river soon enough. King Hiram, with the barons' oaths of loyalty still fresh and new, and the kingdom awash with love for its heroic crown princess, had decided not to abdicate, though I suspected a union of the two crowns would come soon enough; Hiram was not a well man. Dugald and Eleanor were returning to Cragroyal the next day, though they would make a slow progress of it, wandering from castle to castle, village to village, to allow the people to see their new queen. I, curse the luck, was sailing back to Hallaland. The agent following Master Arvol had disappeared somewhere on the road to Rona and so had Master Arvol. My lord, however, was heading for Greyrock Castle and his new duties. Warden of Greyrock meant governor of the scattered folk of the Westwood, as well as guardian of the Greyrock Pass and lord of Greyrock Town.

The Nightwalkers had already gone, save for Aljess and Lord Romner. Aljess was taking her role as Maurey's captain very seriously, and a good thing too, because I would not gamble his life on all the human burghers of Greyrock Town being happy with a Nightwalker overlord. Romner was still closeted in the peace and quiet of an attic room, copying Master Arvol's papers, stolen so long ago in Hallasbourg.

He had finally gotten over his outrage that I had killed Sawfield, robbing him of his long-dreamed-of vengeance for his father's death in the baron's dungeon. (He didn't find it amusing when I pointed out that Aljess too had lost a parent to Sawfield; there wouldn't have been enough of the baron to go round.) Romner was our best hope for breaking the cipher Arvol had used to hide his most secret notes. Alchemists tended to use personal variations of common alchemical ciphers to hide the details of their experiments, and Romner had made a great study of human work in alchemy. That was why he was also the one stuck with trying to figure out what Lady Katerina had been brewing up to use against the Nightwalkers she thought were coming for King Hiram. Moth-repellent, my foot, had been Romner's opinion. All he could say was that it wasn't philosopher's fire, though it might, when complete, be something like the poison that had burned Maurey in the Hallasbourg library. But people who were trying some recipe they had chanced across usually kept a copy to refer to, and Katerina had possessed no written notes at all. She had known exactly what she was doing, and I knew she had lied in most of what she claimed. Her mind swam in lies, that one. Pity we couldn't question her.

"So what do we do about Lady Katerina?" I asked. "You didn't have any luck talking Dugald out of taking her to Cragroyal, Maurey?"

My lord shook his head, carefully moving *Cuin's Life of Blessed Miron* further from the inkhorn. I'd been copying the design of Katerina's medallion and the one I'd taken from the dead man in Hallasbourg library, as well as Arvol's drawing. The short lines joining the seven circles seemed important. In all three they were in the same place between each ring. When Maurey had come back from seeing Dugald at the palace, shedding Aljess in the hall downstairs to oversee his packing, I had been trying to draw the tattoo I had seen on the dead man's hand in the vision, the tattoo the mountain witch-girl had seen. It was difficult to remember it exactly; I thought it was the same, but I might have just been replacing what was there with what I had seen through my own eyes on other occasions. I'd look a right fool if I tore up the Westwood to find those two girls, and they told me the tattoo on the man they killed was just the round, half-black, half-white disc of Mayn the Moon. I dipped my quill and tried again, this time with my eyes shut.

"Eleanor pleaded for Katerina. He gave in. I won't come between Dugald and his wife."

"For *her* safety," said Annot. "For his! Maurey, you can't let Eleanor take that vicious little weasel back to Cragroyal."

"I can't stop her."

"I could," I muttered, opening my eyes. Wonderful. I'd drawn a blobby sort of upside-down pear shape, wandering half off the edge of the paper. Annot sighed and plucked the pen from my hand, as if I were the little boy she used to have to keep down from high trees and out of the duckpond back when a few years' difference in age seemed half a lifetime.

She carefully added ears and stick legs, dotting in eyes and nose: a cross-eyed sheep, its head lowered quizzically.

Maurey took the pen away from us both and flipped the lid closed on the inkhorn. He looked a little exasperated. I can't think why. I wiped my inky hand on my hose.

"We're not murderers," he said.

"But she is," said Annot. "In her heart at least, she is. She's certainly a traitor to her mistress. She was a spy for Sawfield, maybe a spy for the Hallalanders. Eleanor said that was why her mother the queen allowed Katerina to be her friend, because she was a spy. So she betrayed Eleanor from the start; she betrayed Queen Elinda by letting Sawfield buy her and then betrayed

Eleanor again. She denies that she ever suspected Lovell had been murdered to start it all, and we can believe that or not—"

"That's almost the only truth she's said," I muttered.

"But she tried to kill you, Maurey! Even Eleanor admits that."

"She wasn't any real danger," Maurey pointed out.

"She certainly doesn't *seem* like the fearsome assassin she thinks she is," I conceded. "She's no warrior and she's useless in the wilderness, to judge by her performance. But it might be just that, a performance, an act. She's hiding so many secrets."

"She doesn't have to be good to be a danger to Dugald," said Annot, adding as an afterthought, "and to Eleanor. A lady-in-waiting gets everywhere. She'd be alone with them; they'd be unarmed…Look, the two of you are supposed to be keeping Dugald safe, keeping Dunmorra safe. Don't let Katerina walk right into Dunmorra's heart this way." She picked up one of the seven-circled amulets from the table and swung it on her finger. "You know why Lady Katerina is wearing mourning?"

"For Prince Lovell?" I asked.

"Some intelligencer you are, O Master Spy. No, it's for her uncle. One of her mother-who-isn't-a-Penitent's younger brothers."

"How do you know that?"

"I asked. I gushed, 'Oh, poor darling, what a terrible time you've had, and when you've lost someone dear to you'…" Annot whirled the amulet on its ribbon. It flew off, and I snatched it from the air. "Sorry. Go on, dear coz. Ask what happened to the uncle."

I had a sudden idea where this was going. "What happened to the uncle?" I asked obediently.

"Murdered last spring. Innocently strolling along a street near the university, attacked by footpads, left dead in an alley."

"When last spring?"

"Oh, about the time people were breaking into Hallasbourg University library, I think. She only found the letter with news of his death waiting for her when Sawfield brought her back to Rensey."

I picked up the second amulet. "Should we send a herald to investigate Katerina's mother's family? Family histories…maybe this is some forgotten family badge after all."

"Which brings us back to what we should do about Katerina."

"I'm making arrangements," said Maurey. I recognized the tone of voice. That wasn't the shy scholar who drifted around the background of Dugald's court. That was the head of Dugald's intelligence service, the man few people even knew existed, though in Greyrock they were about to find out, I rather suspected.

"I want Lady Ursula, Annot."

"You break my heart." Annot reeled backwards in her chair, hands clasped to her chest.

"Idiot," he said affectionately.

"A bodyguard-in-waiting?"

"She and Lady Joanna, Captain Lord Anders' sister—she's another one like your Lady Ursula, who has some skill with weapons, and a quick mind. And Korby, one of yours, maybe your niece? A witch and a warrior, someone who can act the lady, since we don't want to give the Eswyns a chance to take offence and say we've surrounded their princess with shepherds and cattle thieves."

"Will Dugald agree to assigning Eleanor ladies-in-waiting who are going to be spying on her, or on her best friend, I mean?" Annot asked, before I could retort to the cattle thief insult.

"He did, yes. That's what I was seeing him about."

"Rat. You knew what you were doing all along."

"I usually do, yes." They grinned at one another. "But I

always like to hear what you two think. When you make the effort to."

"You've been talking with Romner too much," Annot said. "You're starting to sound like him. Still, I'm glad you didn't ask me to be a watchdog for you. I almost offered, but I hate being tied down at court…"

"The Eswyns wouldn't be happy with you as their princess's lady, either."

"No," said Annot. "I suppose not."

I broke the suddenly awkward mood, gathering up my scribbles, handing one to each of them. I'd marked the colors of the enamel, the nicks of wear in the silver. Who knew what might actually be important. "Give one to Romner too. He's always saying he has the oldest library in all Eswiland in that crumbling old castle of his in the South Quartering: he can look in it for Yehillons. And see if you can find the body I had that vision of. Even if the tattoo is rotted by now"—Annot made a face—"there might be something in the man's purse, or a cloak-clasp or something, that would give us a clue to who those men were, where they came from and why they attacked that family. And find those witch-girls, Eleanor's outlaws…" Maurey was looking like a university Master Alchemist listening to a boy who'd just discovered that ash and vinegar go *fizz*, and Annot was rolling her eyes. I grinned. "Right. I suppose the kingdom can manage without me for a few months…My ship's catching the turn of the tide downriver and I'd better get going. You look after my horses, Oakhold. Look after one another."

"Look after Maurey, you mean. You never worry about me."

"You're going to Greyrock?"

"For the autumn."

"Don't you have a barony to look after?"

"Don't you have a swamp?" She jumped up and hugged me.

"Take care, Korby. I don't like any of this. This Yehillon thing cropping up now, just when Nightwalkers are starting to come from behind the mountains again. Given the books Arvol was using, they—it, whatever the Yehillon is—must be old, old, old. Something lying in wait, preparing itself. Something that was using King Hallow, maybe, when he conquered Eswiland."

"Using Miron the Burner," said Maurey quietly, "the man who suddenly invented philosopher's fire. Yes."

"We think we're laying the foundation of a new future, building a land where Nightwalkers and humans can live together again like Eswiland was once, if you believe Fen tales," said Annot, "but maybe something's been waiting all this time to prevent that, and we've just woken it up to bring war and fire sweeping over the island again to destroy us all; maybe this time it won't stop at the Talverdin Mountains, now that everyone knows there are ways of getting through the Greyrock Pass."

"Or other passes…"

Valley like a knife-slash, pointing to Talverdin…

Maurey gave me a keen look, but the moment had passed. I shrugged. "So we have to do a better job of stopping them this time, before they have an army. Don't borrow trouble."

Annot let me go and saluted me, mocking, but her words weren't. Nor was the worry in her eyes. "The Powers go with you, Korby."

I belted on my sword and gathered up my bundle. Dugald's fast ship was waiting on me and me alone, but if I made the captain miss the tide so that we couldn't sail till sometime in the small hours of the night, the man would make snide comments about landsmen for the whole five or six days the eastbound crossing could be expected to take.

"My lord."

Maurey embraced me too and stepped back, his hands on my shoulders. "Watch yourself. You have the speaking stone?"

"Yes, I do."

He nodded and said, as Annot had, "The Powers be with you."

"And with you." Though the Powers are more likely to be with the best swordsman, in my experience.

"Don't get yourself killed," he said. "I want you back."

"As my lord commands."

They didn't come with me to the harbor. We didn't want any stir, anyone taking note that members of Dugald's court were slipping away to the continent. I looked back before the porter closed the street door on me and saw the prince and Annot standing together, his arm around her shoulders. Then I turned and strode away.

It was the strangest thing I'd ever set off hunting. A man, a religion, a family, an alchemical formula, a philosophy, a legend…Whatever the Yehillon was, I was starting to believe it threatened all I loved, friends and kin and the whole blood-soaked island my people had lost so long ago.

We're the old blood, we Fenlanders, we witches. We failed the Nightwalkers once, when we lost the land to Hallow.

I owed my lord my life and soul. My people owed the Nightwalkers for their old failure. It would happen again over my dead body.

"If one book has shaped what I think a book should do and what literature should be," medieval scholar K.V. Johansen says, "it is *Lord of the Rings*." As Tolkien was, she is thorough in her research as she creates other worlds for her stories. Readers will find themselves richly rewarded. Johansen lives in a bit of another world herself; she grows exotic trees indoors and seedling oaks and apples outdoors in what used to be the vegetable garden, and hopes some day to have her very own forest, because both the house and the yard are getting rather crowded.

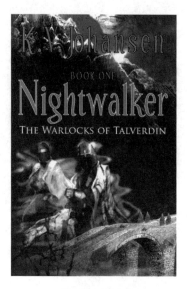

Book One

Nightwalker

The Warlocks of Talverdin

978-1-55143-481-0 $9.95 CDN • $8.95 US PB

Coming soon! The third book in this exciting series:

Book Three

Warden of Greyrock:

The Warlocks of Talverdin

Also by K.V. Johansen

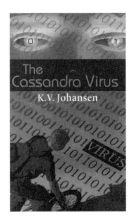

The Cassandra Virus

978-1-55143-497-1 $8.95 CDN • $7.95 US PB